Acclaim for **CHITRA BANERJEE DIVAKARUNI**'s

THE UNKNOWN ERRORS
OF OUR LIVES

CHITRA BANERJEE DIVAKARUNI

THE UNKNOWN ERRORS
OF OUR LIVES

Chitra Banerjee Divakaruni is the bestselling author of the novels *The Mistress of Spices, Sister of My Heart,* and *The Vine of Desire;* the story collection *Arranged Marriage,* which received several awards, including the American Book Award; and four collections of prize-winning poetry. Her work has appeared in *The New Yorker, The Atlantic Monthly, Ms., The Best American Short Stories 1999,* and other publications. Born in India, she lives in the San Francisco area.

THE UNKNOWN ERRORS
OF OUR LIVES

ANCHOR BOOKS

A Division of Random House, Inc.

New York

THE

UNKNOWN

ERRORS

OF OUR

LIVES

Stories by

CHITRA BANERJEE DIVAKARUNI

FIRST ANCHOR BOOKS EDITION, JANUARY 2002

The following stories have previously appeared and are reprinted by permission of the author: "Mrs. Dutta Writes a Letter," *The Atlantic Monthly*, 1999 and *The Best American Short Stories 1999*; "The Forgotten Children," *Sun*, 1995 and *Gulf Coast*, 2000; "The Love of a Good Man," *Good Housekeeping*, 1998; "The Blooming Season for Cacti," *Zoetrope*, 2000; "The Intelligence of Wild Things" (published as "Crossing"), *Weber Review*, 1998; "The Unknown Errors of Our Lives," *Prairie Schooner*, Spring 2001; "The Lives of Strangers," *Agni*, April 2001.

The Library of Congress has cataloged the Doubleday edition as follows:
Divakaruni, Chitra Banerjee, 1956–
The unknown errors of our lives : stories / by Chitra Banerjee Divakaruni.—1st ed.
p. cm.
ISBN 0-385-49727-X
Contents: Mrs. Dutta writes a letter—The intelligence of wild things—The lives of strangers—The love of a good man—What the body knows—The forgotten children—The blooming season for cacti—The unknown errors of our lives—The names of stars in Bengali.
1. United States—Social life and customs—20th century—Fiction. 2. India—Social life and customs—Fiction. 3. East Indian Americans—Fiction. I. Title.
PS3554.I86 U5 2001
813'.54—dc21
00-047509
CIP

Anchor ISBN: 0-385-49728-8

Book design by Gretchen Achilles

www.anchorbooks.com

Printed in the United States of America
10 9 8 7 6 5 4 3 2 1

TO MY THREE MEN:

Abhay,

Anand,

Murthy

ACKNOWLEDGMENTS

MY DEEPEST THANKS TO:

My agent, Sandra Dijkstra, for the battles she fights on my behalf

My editor, Deb Futter, for guidance, encouragement, and vision

Michael Curtis, Jhumpa Lahiri, Dean Nelson, Susanne Pari, Amy Tan, and Latha Viswanathan, for helping these stories find their shape and place

My mother, Tatini Banerjee, and my mother-in-law, Sita Divakaruni, for blessings and belief

Murthy, Anand, and Abhay, for putting up with all my errors

Gurumayi Chidvilasananda and Swami Chinmayananda for Grace

"Who you are is a mystery no one can answer,
not even you."

—JAMAICA KINCAID, *The Autobiography of My Mother*

"the desire to touch
the desire to speak . . .

i could love her standing in the doorway,
thinking she's made the wrong choice"

—TOI DERRICOTTE, *Tender*

CONTENTS

THE UNKNOWN ERRORS
OF OUR LIVES

MR/. DUTTA
WRITE/ A LETTER

WHEN THE ALARM goes off at 5:00 A.M., buzzing like a trapped wasp, Mrs. Dutta has been lying awake for quite a while. Though it has now been two months, she still has difficulty sleeping on the Perma Rest mattress Sagar and Shyamoli, her son and daughter-in-law, have bought specially for her. It is too American-soft, unlike the reassuringly solid copra ticking she is used to at home. *Except this is home now,* she reminds herself. She reaches hurriedly to turn off the alarm, but in the dark her fingers get confused among the knobs, and the electric clock falls with a thud to the floor. Its insistent metallic call vibrates out through the walls of her room until she is sure it will wake everyone. She yanks frantically at the wire until she feels it give, and in the abrupt silence that follows she hears herself breathing, a sound harsh and uneven and full of guilt.

Mrs. Dutta knows, of course, that this turmoil is her own fault. She should just not set the alarm. There is no need for her to get up early here in Sunnyvale, in her son's house. But the habit, taught to her by her mother-in-law when she was a bride of seventeen, *a good wife wakes before the rest of the household,* is one she finds impossible to break. How hard it was then to pull her unwilling body away from her husband's sleep-warm clasp, Sagar's father whom she had just learned to love. To stumble to the kitchen that smelled of stale garam masala and light the coal unoon so she could make morning tea for them all—her parents-in-law, her husband, his two younger brothers, the widow aunt who lived with them.

After dinner, when the family sits in front of the TV, she attempts to tell her grandchildren about those days. "I was never good at starting that unoon—the smoke stung my eyes, making me cough and cough. Breakfast was never ready on time, and my mother-in-law—oh, how she scolded me until I was in tears. Every night I would pray to Goddess Durga, please let me sleep late, just one morning!"

"Mmmm," Pradeep says, bent over a model plane.

"Oooh, how awful," says Mrinalini, wrinkling her nose politely before she turns back to a show filled with jokes that Mrs. Dutta does not understand.

"That's why you should sleep in now, Mother," says Shyamoli, smiling from the recliner where she sits looking through the *Wall Street Journal*. With her legs crossed so elegantly under the shimmery blue skirt she has changed into after work, and her unusually fair skin, she could pass for an American, thinks Mrs. Dutta, whose own skin is brown as roasted cumin. The thought fills her with an uneasy pride.

From the floor where he leans against Shyamoli's knee, Sagar adds, "We want you to be comfortable, Ma. To rest. That's why we brought you to America."

In spite of his thinning hair and the gold-rimmed glasses which he has recently taken to wearing, Sagar's face seems to Mrs. Dutta still that of the boy she used to send off to primary school with his metal tiffin box. She remembers how he crawled into her bed on stormy monsoon nights, how when he was ill no one else could make him drink his barley water. Her heart balloons in sudden gladness because she is really here, with him and his children in America. "Oh, Sagar"—she smiles—now you're talking like this! But did you give me a moment's rest while you were growing up?" And she launches into a description of childhood pranks that has him shaking his head indulgently while disembodied TV laughter echoes through the room.

But later he comes into her bedroom and says, a little shamefaced, "Mother, please, don't get up so early in the morning. All that noise in the bathroom, it wakes us up, and Molli has such a long day at work . . ."

And she, turning a little so he shouldn't see her foolish eyes filling with tears as though she were a teenage bride again and not a woman well over sixty, nods her head, *yes, yes.*

WAITING FOR THE sounds of the stirring household to release her from the embrace of her Perma Rest mattress, Mrs. Dutta repeats the 108 holy names of God. *Om Keshavaya Namah, Om Narayanaya Namah, Om Madhavaya Namah.* But underneath she is thinking of the bleached-blue aerogram from Mrs. Basu that has been waiting unanswered on her bedside table all week, filled with news from home. There was a robbery at Sandhya Jewelry Store, the bandits had guns but luckily no one was hurt. Mr. Joshi's daughter, that sweet-faced child, has run away with her singing teacher, who would've thought it. Mrs. Barucha's daughter-in-law had one more baby girl, yes, their fourth, you'd think they'd know better than to keep trying for a boy. Last

Tuesday was Bangla Bandh, another labor strike, everything closed down, even the buses not running, but you can't really blame them, can you, after all factory workers have to eat, too. Mrs. Basu's tenants, whom she'd been trying to evict forever, had finally moved out, good riddance, but you should see the state of the flat.

At the very bottom Mrs. Basu wrote, *Are you happy in America?*

Mrs. Dutta knows that Mrs. Basu, who has been her closest friend since they both came to Ghoshpara Lane as young brides, cannot be fobbed off with descriptions of Fisherman's Wharf and the Golden Gate Bridge, or even anecdotes involving grandchildren. And so she has been putting off her reply while in her heart family loyalty battles with insidious feelings of—but she turns from them quickly and will not name them even to herself.

Now Sagar is knocking on the children's doors—a curious custom, this, children being allowed to close their doors against their parents—and with relief Mrs. Dutta gathers up her bathroom things. She has plenty of time. It will take a second rapping from their mother before Pradeep and Mrinalini open their doors and stumble out. Still, she is not one to waste the precious morning. She splashes cold water on her face and neck (she does not believe in pampering herself), scrapes the night's gumminess from her

tongue with her metal tongue cleaner, and brushes vigorously, though the minty toothpaste does not leave her
mouth feeling as clean as did the bittersweet neem stick
she'd been using all her life. She combs the knots out of
her hair. Even at her age, it is thicker and silkier than her
daughter-in-law's permed curls. *Such vanity*, she scolds her
reflection, *and you a grandmother and a widow besides*. Still,
as she deftly fashions her hair into a neat coil, she remembers how her husband would always compare it to night
rain.

She hears a commotion outside.

"Pat! Minnie! What d'you mean you still haven't
washed up? I'm late every morning to work nowadays because of you kids."

"But, Mom, *she's* in there. She's been there forever..."
says Mrinalini.

Pause. Then, "So go to the downstairs bathroom."

"But all our stuff is here," says Pradeep, and Mrinalini
adds, "It's not fair. Why can't *she* go downstairs?"

A longer pause. Inside the bathroom Mrs. Dutta hopes
Shyamoli will not be too harsh on the girl. But a child who
refers to elders in that disrespectful way ought to be pun-
ished. How many times had she slapped Sagar for something far less, though he was her only one, the jewel of her
eye, come to her after she had been married for seven years

and everyone had given up hope already? Whenever she lifted her hand to him it was as though her heart was being put through a masala grinder. Such is a mother's duty.

But Shyamoli only says, in a tired voice, "That's enough! Go put on your clothes, hurry."

The grumblings recede. Footsteps clatter down the stairs. Inside the bathroom Mrs. Dutta bends over the sink, gripping the folds of her sari. Hard to think through the pounding in her head to what it is she feels most—anger at the children for their rudeness, or at Shyamoli for letting them go unrebuked. Or is it shame that clogs her throat, stinging, sulfuric, indigestible?

IT IS 9.00 A.M. and the house, after the flurry of departures, of frantic "I can't find my socks," and "Mom, he took my lunch money," and "I swear I'll leave you kids behind if you're not in the car in exactly one minute," has settled into its placid daytime rhythms.

Busy in the kitchen, Mrs. Dutta has recovered her spirits. It is too exhausting to hold on to grudges, and, besides, the kitchen—sunlight sliding across its countertops while the refrigerator hums reassuringly—is her favorite place.

Mrs. Dutta hums too as she fries potatoes for alu dum. Her voice is rusty and slightly off-key. In India she would never have ventured to sing, but with everyone gone, the house is too quiet, all that silence pressing down on her like the heel of a giant hand, and the TV voices, with their unreal accents, are no help at all. As the potatoes turn golden-brown, she permits herself a moment of nostalgia for her Calcutta kitchen—the new gas stove bought with the birthday money Sagar sent, the scoured brass pots stacked by the meat safe, the window with the lotus-pattern grille through which she could look down on children playing cricket after school. The mouth-watering smell of ginger and chili paste, ground fresh by Reba the maid, and, in the evening, strong black Assam cha brewing in the kettle when Mrs. Basu came by to visit. In her mind she writes to Mrs. Basu, *Oh, Roma, I miss it all so much, sometimes I feel that someone has reached in and torn out a handful of my chest.*

But only fools indulge in nostalgia, so Mrs. Dutta shakes her head clear of images and straightens up the kitchen. She pours the half-drunk glasses of milk down the sink, though Shyamoli has told her to save them in the refrigerator. But surely Shyamoli, a girl from a good Hindu family, doesn't expect her to put contaminated jutha things in with the rest of the food? She washes the breakfast dishes by hand instead of letting them wait inside the dishwater till night, breeding germs. With practiced fingers she throws an assortment of spices into the blender: coriander, cumin, cloves, black pepper, a few red chilies for vigor. No stale bottled curry powder for *her! At least the family's eating well since I arrived,* she writes in her mind, *proper Indian food, rutis that puff up the way they should, fish curry in mustard sauce, and real pulao with raisins and cashews and ghee—the way you taught me, Roma—instead of Rice-a-roni.* She would like to add, *They love it,* but thinking of Shyamoli she hesitates.

At first Shyamoli had been happy enough to have someone take over the cooking. It's wonderful to come home to a hot dinner, she'd say, or, Mother, what crispy papads, and your fish gravy is out of this world. But recently she's taken to picking at her food, and once or twice from the kitchen Mrs. Dutta has caught wisps of words, intensely whispered: *cholesterol, all putting on weight, she's spoiling you.* And though Shyamoli always refuses when the children ask if they can have burritos from the freezer instead, Mrs. Dutta suspects that she would really like to say yes.

THE CHILDREN. A heaviness pulls at Mrs. Dutta's entire body when she thinks of them. Like so much in this country they have turned out to be—yes, she might as well admit it—a disappointment.

For this she blames, in part, the Olan Mills portrait. Perhaps it had been impractical of her to set so much store on a photograph, especially one taken years ago. But it was such a charming scene—Mrinalini in a ruffled white dress with her arm around her brother, Pradeep chubby and dimpled in a suit and bow tie, a glorious autumn forest blazing red and yellow behind them. (Later Mrs. Dutta would learn, with a sense of having been betrayed, that the forest was merely a backdrop in a studio in California, where real trees did not turn such colors.)

The picture had arrived, silver-framed and wrapped in a plastic sheet filled with bubbles, with a note from Shyamoli explaining that it was a Mother's Day gift. (A strange concept, a day set aside to honor mothers. Did the sahebs not honor their mothers the rest of the year, then?) For a week Mrs. Dutta could not decide where it should be hung. If she put it in the drawing room, visitors would be able to admire her grandchildren, but if she put it on the bedroom wall, she would be able to see the photo, last thing, before she fell asleep. She had finally opted for the bedroom, and later, when she was too ill with pneumonia to leave her bed for a month, she'd been glad of it.

Mrs. Dutta was not unused to living on her own. She had done it for the last three years, since Sagar's father died, politely but stubbornly declining the offers of various relatives, well-meaning and otherwise, to come and stay with her. In this she had surprised herself as well as others, who thought of her as a shy, sheltered woman, one who would surely fall apart without her husband to handle things for her. But she managed quite well. She missed Sagar's father, of course, especially in the evenings, when it had been his habit to read to her the more amusing parts of the newspaper while she rolled out rutis. But once the grief receded, she found it rather pleasant to be mistress of her own life, as she confided to Mrs. Basu. She liked being able, for the first time ever, to lie in bed all evening and read a new novel of Shankar's straight through if she wanted, or to send out for hot brinjal pakoras on a rainy day without feeling guilty that she wasn't serving up a balanced meal.

When the pneumonia hit, everything changed.

Mrs. Dutta had been ill before, but those illnesses had been different. Even in bed she'd been at the center of the household, with Reba coming to find out what should be cooked, Sagar's father bringing her shirts with missing buttons, her mother-in-law, now old and tamed, complaining that the cook didn't brew her tea strong enough, and Sagar running in crying because he'd had a fight with the neighbor boy. But now there was no one to ask her, querulously, *Just how long do you plan to remain sick,* no one waiting in impatient exasperation for her to take on her duties again, no one whose life was inconvenienced the least bit by her illness.

There was, therefore, no reason for her to get well.

When this thought occurred to Mrs. Dutta, she was so frightened that her body grew numb. The walls of the room spun into blackness, the bed on which she lay, a vast four-poster she had shared with Sagar's father since her marriage, rocked like a mastless dinghy caught in a storm, and a great, muted roar reverberated in the cavities of her skull. For a moment, unable to move or see, she thought, *I'm dead.* Then her vision, desperate and blurry, caught on the portrait. *My grandchildren.* She focused, with some difficulty, on the bright, oblivious sheen of their child faces, the eyes so like Sagar's that for a moment she could feel heartsickness cramping her joints like arthritis. She drew in a shuddering breath; the roaring seemed to recede. When the afternoon post brought another letter from Sagar, *Mother, you really should come and live with us, we worry about you all alone in India, especially when you're sick like this,* she wrote back the same day, with fingers that still shook a little, *You're right, my place is with you, with my grandchildren.*

But now that she is here on the other side of the world, she is wrenched by doubt. She knows the grandchildren love her—how can it be otherwise among family? And she loves them, she reminds herself, though they have put away, somewhere in the back of a closet, the vellum-bound *Ramayana for Young Readers* that she carried all the way from

India in her hand luggage. Though their bodies twitch with impatience when she tries to tell them stories of her girl-hood. Though they offer the most transparent excuses when she asks them to sit with her while she chants the evening arati. *They're flesh of my flesh, blood of my blood,* she reminds herself. But sometimes when she listens, from the other room, to them speaking on the phone, their American voices rising in excitement as they discuss a glittering alien world of Power Rangers, Spice Girls, and Spirit Week at school, she almost cannot believe it.

STEPPING INTO THE backyard with a bucket of newly washed clothes, Mrs. Dutta views the sky with some anxi-ety. The butter-gold sunlight is gone, black-bellied clouds have taken over the horizon, and the air feels still and heavy on her face, as before a Bengal storm. What if her clothes don't dry by the time the others return home?

Washing clothes has been a problem for Mrs. Dutta ever since she arrived in California.

"We can't, Mother," Shyamoli had said with a sigh when Mrs. Dutta asked Sagar to put up a clothesline for her in the backyard. (Shyamoli sighed often nowadays. Perhaps it was an American habit? Mrs. Dutta did not re-member the Indian Shyamoli, the docile bride she'd mothered for a month before putting her on a Pan Am flight to join her husband, pursing her lips in quite this way to let out a breath at once patient and vexed.) "It's just not *done*, not in a nice neighborhood like this one. And being the only Indian family on the street, we have to be extra careful. People here, sometimes—." She'd broken off with a shake of her head. "Why don't you just keep your dirty clothes in the hamper I've put in your room, and I'll wash them on Sunday along with everyone else's."

Afraid of causing another sigh, Mrs. Dutta had agreed reluctantly. But she knew she should not store unclean clothes in the same room where she kept the pictures of her gods. That brought bad luck. And the odor. Lying in bed at night she could smell it distinctly, even though Shyamoli claimed the hamper was airtight. The sour, starchy old-woman smell embarrassed her.

What embarrassed her more was when, Sunday afternoons, Shyamoli brought the laundry into the family room to fold. Mrs. Dutta would bend intensely over her knitting, face tingling with shame, as her daughter-in-law nonchalantly shook out the wisps of lace, magenta and sea-green and black, that were her panties, laying them next to a stack of Sagar's briefs. And when, right in front of everyone, Shyamoli pulled out Mrs. Dutta's own crumpled, baggy bras from the clothes heap, she wished the ground would open up and swallow her, like the Sita of mythology.

Then one day Shyamoli set the clothes basket down in front of Sagar.

"Can you do them today, Sagar?" (Mrs. Dutta, who had never, through the forty-two years of her marriage, addressed Sagar's father by name, tried not to wince.) "I've got to get that sales report into the computer by tonight."

Before Sagar could respond, Mrs. Dutta was out of her chair, knitting needles dropping to the floor.

"No no no, clothes and all is no work for the man of the house. I'll do it." The thought of her son's hands searching through the basket and lifting up his wife's—and her own—underclothes filled her with horror.

"Mother!" Shyamoli said. "This is why Indian men are so useless around the house. Here in America we don't believe in men's work and women's work. Don't I work outside all day, just like Sagar? How'll I manage if he doesn't help me at home?"

"I'll help you instead," Mrs. Dutta ventured.

"You don't understand, do you, Mother?" Shyamoli said with a shaky smile. Then she went into the study.

Mrs. Dutta sat down in her chair and tried to understand. But after a while she gave up and whispered to Sagar that she wanted him to teach her how to run the washer and dryer.

"Why, Mother? Molli's quite happy to . . ."

"I've got to learn it. . . ." Her voice warped with distress as she rummaged through the tangled heap for her clothes.

Her son began to object, then shrugged. "Oh very well. If that's what you really want."

But later, when she faced them alone, the machines with their cryptic symbols and rows of gleaming knobs terrified her. What if she pressed the wrong button and flooded the entire floor with soapsuds? What if she couldn't turn the machines off and they kept going, whirring maniacally, until they exploded? (This had happened to a woman on a TV show just the other day, and she had jumped up and down, screaming. Everyone else found it hilarious, but Mrs. Dutta sat stiff-spined, gripping the armrest of her chair.) So she took to washing her clothes in the bathtub when she was alone. She had never done such a chore before, but she remembered how the village washerwomen of her childhood would beat their saris clean against river rocks. And a curious satisfaction filled her as her clothes hit the porcelain with the same solid wet *thunk*.

My small victory, my secret.

This is why everything must be dried and put safely away before Shyamoli returns. Ignorance, as Mrs. Dutta knows well from years of managing a household, is a great promoter of harmony. So she keeps an eye on the menacing advance of the clouds as she hangs up her blouse and underwear. As she drapes her sari along the redwood fence that separates her son's property from the neighbor's, first wiping it clean with a dish towel she has secretly taken from the bottom drawer of the kitchen. But she isn't too worried. Hasn't she managed every time, even after that freak hailstorm last month when she had to use the iron from the laundry closet to press everything dry? The memory pleases her. In her mind she writes to Mrs. Basu, *I'm fitting in so well here, you'd never guess I came only two months back. I've found new ways of doing things, of solving problems creatively. You would be most proud if you saw me.*

WHEN MRS. DUTTA decided to give up her home of forty-five years, her relatives showed far less surprise than she had expected.

"Oh, we all knew you'd end up in America sooner or later," they said. "It was a foolishness to stay on alone so long after Sagar's father, may he find eternal peace, passed away. Good thing that boy of yours came to his senses and called you to join him. Everyone knows a wife's place is with her husband, and a widow's with her son."

Mrs. Dutta had nodded meek agreement, ashamed to let anyone know that the night before she had awakened weeping.

"Well, now that you're going, what'll happen to all your things?"

Mrs. Dutta, still troubled over those treacherous tears, had offered up her household effects in propitiation. "Here, Didi, you take this cutwork bedspread. Mashima, for a long time I meant for you to have these Corning Ware dishes, I know how much you admire them. And, Boudi, this tape recorder that Sagar sent a year back is for you. Yes yes, I'm quite sure. I can always tell Sagar to buy me another one when I get there."

Mrs. Basu, coming in just as a cousin made off triumphantly with a bone china tea set, had protested. "Prameela, have you gone crazy? That tea set used to belong to your mother-in-law."

"But what'll I do with it in America? Shyamoli has her own set—"

A look that Mrs. Dutta couldn't read flitted across Mrs. Basu's face. "But do you want to drink from it for the rest of your life?"

"What do you mean?"

Mrs. Basu hesitated. Then she said, "What if you don't like it there?"

"How can I not like it, Roma?" Mrs. Dutta's voice was strident, even to her own ears. With an effort she controlled it and continued, "I'll miss my friends, I know—and you

most of all. The things we do together—evening tea, our
walk around Rabindra Sarobar Lake, Thursday night Bha-
gavat Geeta class. But Sagar—they're my only family. And
blood is blood after all."

"I wonder," Mrs. Basu said dryly, and Mrs. Dutta re-
called that though both of Mrs. Basu's children lived just a
day's journey away, they came to see her only on occasions
when common decency demanded their presence. Perhaps
they were tightfisted in money matters too. Perhaps that
was why Mrs. Basu had started renting out her downstairs
a few years ago, even though, as anyone in Calcutta knew,
tenants were more trouble than they were worth. Such filial neglect must be hard to take, though Mrs. Basu, loyal to
her children as indeed a mother should be, never com-
plained. In a way Mrs. Dutta had been better off, with
Sagar too far away for her to put his love to the test.

"At least don't give up the house," Mrs. Basu was saying. "It'll be impossible to find another place in case—"

"In case what?" Mrs. Dutta asked, her words like stone
chips. She was surprised to find that she was angrier with
Mrs. Basu than she'd ever been. Or was it fear? *My son isn't
like yours,* she'd been on the verge of spitting out. She took
a deep breath and made herself smile, made herself remember that she might never see her friend again.

"Ah, Roma," she said, putting her arm around Mrs.

Basu, "you think I'm such an old witch that my Sagar and my Shyamoli will be unable to live with me?"

MRS. DUTTA HUMS a popular Rabindra Sangeet as she pulls her sari from the fence. It's been a good day, as good as it can be in a country where you might stare out the window for hours and not see one living soul. No vegetable vendors with wicker baskets balanced on their heads, no knife-sharpeners calling *scissors-knives-choppers, scissors-knives-choppers* to bring the children running. No dehati women with tattoos on their arms to sell you cookware in exchange for your old silk saris. Why, even the animals that frequented Ghoshpara Lane had personality. Stray dogs that knew to line up outside the kitchen door just when leftovers were likely to be thrown out, the goat who maneuvered its head through the garden grille hoping to get at her dahlias, cows who planted themselves majestically in the center of the road, ignoring honking drivers. And right across the street was Mrs. Basu's two-story house, which Mrs. Dutta knew as well as her own. How many times had she walked up the stairs to that airy room painted sea-green and filled with plants where her friend would be waiting for her.

What took you so long today, Prameela? Your tea is cold already.

Wait till you hear what happened, Roma. Then you won't scold me for being late. . . .

Stop it, you silly woman, Mrs. Dutta tells herself severely. Every single one of your relatives would give an arm and a leg to be in your place, you know that. After lunch you're going to write a nice, long letter to Roma, telling her exactly how delighted you are to be here.

From where Mrs. Dutta stands, gathering up petticoats and blouses, she can look into the next yard. Not that there's much to see, just tidy grass and a few pale-blue flowers whose name she doesn't know. There are two wooden chairs under a tree, but Mrs. Dutta has never seen anyone using them. What's the point of having such a big yard if you're not even going to sit in it? she thinks. Calcutta pushes itself into her mind again, Calcutta with its narrow, blackened flats where families of six and eight and ten squeeze themselves into two tiny rooms, and her heart fills with a sense of loss she knows to be illogical.

When she first arrived in Sagar's home, Mrs. Dutta wanted to go over and meet her next-door neighbors, maybe take them some of her special rose-water rasogollahs, as she'd often done with Mrs. Basu. But Shyamoli said she shouldn't. Such things were not the custom in California, she explained earnestly. You didn't just drop in on people without calling ahead. Here everyone was busy, they didn't sit around chatting, drinking endless cups of sugar tea. Why, they might even say something unpleasant to her.

"For what?" Mrs. Dutta had asked disbelievingly, and

Shyamoli had said, "Because Americans don't like neighbors to"—here she used an English phrase—"invade their privacy." Mrs. Dutta, who didn't fully understand the word *privacy* because there was no such term in Bengali, had gazed at her daughter-in-law in some bewilderment. But she understood enough to not ask again. In the following months, though, she often looked over the fence, hoping to make contact. People were people, whether in India or America, and everyone appreciated a friendly face. When Shyamoli was as old as Mrs. Dutta, she would know that, too.

Today, just as she is about to turn away, out of the corner of her eye Mrs. Dutta notices a movement. At one of the windows a woman is standing, her hair a sleek gold like that of the TV heroines whose exploits baffle Mrs. Dutta when sometimes she tunes in to an afternoon serial. She is smoking a cigarette, and a curl of gray rises lazily, elegantly from her fingers. Mrs. Dutta is so happy to see another human being in the middle of her solitary day that she forgets how much she disapproves of smoking, especially in women. She lifts her hand in the gesture she has seen her grandchildren use to wave an eager hello.

The woman stares back at Mrs. Dutta. Her lips are a perfect-painted red, and when she raises her cigarette to her mouth, its tip glows like an animal's eye. She does not wave back or smile. Perhaps she is not well? Mrs. Dutta feels sorry for her, alone in her illness in a silent house with only cigarettes for solace, and she wishes the etiquette of America had not prevented her from walking over with a word of cheer and a bowl of her fresh-cooked alu dum.

MRS. DUTTA RARELY gets a chance to be alone with her son. In the morning he is in too much of a hurry even to drink the fragrant cardamom tea which she (remembering how as a child he would always beg for a sip from her cup) offers to make him. He doesn't return until dinnertime, and afterward he must help the children with their homework, read the paper, hear the details of Shyamoli's day, watch his favorite TV crime show in order to unwind, and take out the garbage. In between, for he is a solicitous son, he converses with Mrs. Dutta. In response to his questions she assures him that her arthritis is much better now; no, no, she's not growing bored being at home all the time; she has everything she needs—Shyamoli has been so kind—but perhaps he could pick up a few aerograms on his way back tomorrow? She recites obediently for him an edited list of her day's activities and smiles when he praises her cooking. But when he says, "Oh, well, time to turn in, another working day tomorrow," she is racked by a vague pain, like hunger, in the region of her heart.

So it is with the delighted air of a child who has been offered an unexpected gift that she leaves her half-written letter to greet Sagar at the door today, a good hour before Shyamoli is due back. The children are busy in the family room doing homework and watching cartoons (mostly the latter, Mrs. Dutta suspects). But for once she doesn't mind because they race in to give their father hurried hugs and then race back again. And she has him, her son, all to herself in a kitchen filled with the familiar, pungent odors of tamarind sauce and chopped coriander leaves.

"Khoka," she says, calling him by the childhood name she hasn't used in years, "I could fry you two-three hot-hot luchis, if you like." As she waits for his reply she can feel, in the hollow of her throat, the rapid beat of her blood. And when he says yes, that would be very nice, she shuts her eyes and takes a deep breath, and it is as though merciful time has given her back her youth, that sweet, aching urgency of being needed again.

MRS. DUTTA IS telling Sagar a story.

"When you were a child, how scared you were of injections! One time, when the government doctor came to give us compulsory typhoid shots, you locked yourself in the bathroom and refused to come out. Do you remember what your father finally did? He went into the garden and caught a lizard and threw it in the bathroom window, because you were even more scared of lizards than of shots. And in exactly one second you ran out screaming—right into the waiting doctor's arms."

Sagar laughs so hard that he almost upsets his tea (made with real sugar, because Mrs. Dutta knows it is better for her son than that chemical powder Shyamoli likes to use). There are tears in his eyes, and Mrs. Dutta, who had not dared to hope he would find her story so amusing, feels gratified. When he takes off his glasses to wipe them, his face is oddly young, not like a father's at all, or even a husband's, and she has to suppress an impulse to put out her hand and rub away the indentations the glasses have left on his nose.

"I'd totally forgotten," says Sagar. "How can you keep track of those old, old things?"

Because it is the lot of mothers to remember what no one else cares to, Mrs. Dutta thinks. To tell them over and over until they are lodged, perforce, in family lore. We are the keepers of the heart's dusty corners.

But as she starts to say this, the front door creaks open, and she hears the faint click of Shyamoli's high heels. Mrs. Dutta rises, collecting the dirty dishes.

"Call me fifteen minutes before you're ready to eat so I can fry fresh luchis for everyone," she tells Sagar.

"You don't have to leave, Mother," he says.

Mrs. Dutta smiles her pleasure but doesn't stop. She knows Shyamoli likes to be alone with her husband at this time, and today in her happiness she does not grudge her this.

"You think I've nothing to do, only sit and gossip with you?" she mock-scolds. "I want you to know I have a very important letter to finish."

Somewhere behind her she hears a thud, a briefcase falling over. This surprises her. Shyamoli is always so careful with her case because it was a gift from Sagar when she was finally made a manager in her company.

"Hi!" Sagar calls, and when there's no answer, "Hey, Molli, you okay?"

Shyamoli comes into the room slowly, her hair disheveled as though she's been running her fingers through it. A hectic color blotches her cheeks.

"What's the matter, Molli?" Sagar walks over to give her a kiss. "Bad day at work?" Mrs. Dutta, embarrassed as always by this display of marital affection, turns toward the window, but not before she sees Shyamoli move her face away.

"Leave me alone." Her voice is wobbly. "Just leave me alone."

"But what is it?" Sagar says in concern.

"I don't want to talk about it right now." Shyamoli

lowers herself into a kitchen chair and puts her face in her hands. Sagar stands in the middle of the room, looking helpless. He raises his hand and lets it fall, as though he wants to comfort his wife but is afraid of what she might do.

A protective anger for her son surges inside Mrs. Dutta, but she leaves the room silently. In her mind-letter she writes, *Women need to be strong, not react to every little thing like this. You and I, Roma, we had far worse to cry about, but we shed our tears invisibly. We were good wives and daughters-in-law, good mothers. Dutiful, uncomplaining. Never putting ourselves first.*

A sudden memory comes to her, one she hasn't thought of in years, a day when she scorched a special kheer dessert. Her mother-in-law had shouted at her, "Didn't your mother teach you anything, you useless girl?" As punishment she refused to let Mrs. Dutta go with Mrs. Basu to the cinema, even though *Sahib, Bibi aur Ghulam*, which all Calcutta was crazy about, was playing, and their tickets were bought already. Mrs. Dutta had wept the entire afternoon, but before Sagar's father came home she washed her face carefully with cold water and applied kajal to her eyes so he wouldn't know.

But everything is getting mixed up, and her own young, trying-not-to-cry face blurs into another—why, it's Shyamoli's—and a thought hits her so sharply in the chest she has to hold on to the bedroom wall. *And what good did it do? The more we bent, the more people pushed us, until one day we'd forgotten that we could stand up straight. Maybe Shyamoli's doing the right thing, after all. . . .*

Mrs. Dutta lowers herself heavily on to her bed, trying to erase such an insidious idea from her mind. Oh, this new country where all the rules are upside down, it's confusing her. Her mind feels muddy, like a pond in which too many water buffaloes have been wading. Maybe things will settle down if she can focus on the letter to Roma.

Then she remembers that she has left the half-written aerogram on the kitchen table. She knows she should wait until after dinner, after her son and his wife have sorted things out. But a restlessness—or is it defiance?—has taken hold of her. She's sorry Shyamoli's upset, but why should she have to waste her evening because of that? She'll go get her letter—it's no crime, is it? She'll march right in and pick it up, and even if Shyamoli stops in midsentence with another one of those sighs, she'll refuse to feel apologetic. Besides, by now they're probably in the family room, watching TV.

Really, Roma, she writes in her head as she feels her way along the unlighted corridor, *the amount of TV they watch here is quite scandalous. The children too, sitting for hours in front of that box like they've been turned into painted Kesto Nagar dolls, and then talking back when I tell them to turn it off.* Of course, she will never put such blasphemy into a real letter. Still, it makes her feel better to say it, if only to herself.

In the family room the TV is on, but for once no one is paying it any attention. Shyamoli and Sagar sit on the sofa, conversing. From where she stands in the corridor, Mrs. Dutta cannot see them, but their shadows—enormous against the wall where the table lamp has cast them—seem to flicker and leap at her.

She is about to slip unseen into the kitchen when Shyamoli's rising voice arrests her. In its raw, shaking un-happiness it is so unlike her daughter-in-law's assured tones that Mrs. Dutta is no more able to move away from it than if she had heard the call of the nishi, the lost souls of the dead on whose tales she grew up.

"It's easy for you to say 'Calm down.' I'd like to see how calm *you'd* be if she came up to you and said, 'Kindly tell the old lady not to hang her clothes over the fence into my yard.' She said it twice, like I didn't understand English, like I was an idiot. All these years I've been so careful not to give these Americans a chance to say something like this, and now—"

"Shhh, Shyamoli, I *said* I'd talk to Mother about it."

"You always say that, but you never *do* anything. You're too busy being the perfect son, tiptoeing around her feel-ings. But how about mine?"

"Hush, Molli, the children . . ."

"Let them hear. I don't care anymore. They're not stupid. They already know what a hard time I've been having with her. You're the only one who refuses to see it."

In the passage Mrs. Dutta shrinks against the wall. She wants to move away, to not hear anything else, but her feet are formed of cement, impossible to lift, and Shyamoli's words pour into her ears like smoking oil.

"I've explained over and over, and she still keeps on doing what I've asked her not to—throwing away perfectly good food, leaving dishes to drip all over the countertops. Ordering my children to stop doing things I've given them permission for. She's taken over the entire kitchen, cooking whatever she likes. You come in the door and the smell of grease is everywhere, in all our clothes. I feel like this isn't my house anymore."

"Be patient, Molli, she's an old woman, after all."

"I know. That's why I tried so hard. I know having her here is important to you. But I can't do it any longer. I just can't. Some days I feel like taking the kids and leaving." Shyamoli's voice disappears into a sob.

A shadow stumbles across the wall to her, and then another. Behind the weatherman's nasal tones announcing a week of sunny days, Mrs. Dutta can hear a high, frightened weeping. The children, she thinks. It's probably the first time they've seen their mother cry.

"Don't talk like that, sweetheart." Sagar leans forward, his voice, too, miserable. All the shadows on the wall shiver and merge into a single dark silhouette.

Mrs. Dutta stares at that silhouette, the solidarity of it. Sagar and Shyamoli's murmurs are lost beneath a noise—is it in her veins, this dry humming, the way the taps in Calcutta used to hum when the municipality turned the water off? After a while she discovers that she has reached her room. In darkness she lowers herself on to her bed very gently, as though her body is made of the thinnest glass. Or perhaps ice, she is so cold. She sits for a long time with her eyes closed, while inside her head thoughts whirl faster and faster until they disappear in a gray dust storm.

WHEN PRADEEP FINALLY comes to call her for dinner, Mrs. Dutta follows him to the kitchen where she fries luchis for everyone, the perfect circles of dough puffing up crisp and golden as always. Sagar and Shyamoli have reached a truce of some kind: she gives him a small smile, and he puts out a casual hand to massage the back of her neck. Mrs. Dutta demonstrates no embarrassment at this. She eats her dinner. She answers questions put to her. She smiles when someone makes a joke. If her face is stiff, as though she has been given a shot of Novocain, no one notices. When the table is cleared, she excuses herself, saying she has to finish her letter.

Now Mrs. Dutta sits on her bed, reading over what she wrote in the innocent afternoon.

Dear Roma,

Although I miss you, I know you will be pleased to hear how happy I am in America. There is much here that needs getting used to, but we are no strangers to adjusting, we old women. After all, haven't we been doing it all our lives?

Today I'm cooking one of Sagar's favorite dishes, alu-dum. . . . It gives me such pleasure to see my family gathered around the table, eating my food. The children are still a little shy of me, but I am hopeful that we'll soon be friends. And Shyamoli, so confident and successful—you should see her when she's all dressed for work. I can't believe she's the same timid bride I sent off to America just a few years ago. But, Sagar, most of all, is the joy of my old age. . . .

With the edge of her sari Mrs. Dutta carefully wipes a tear that has fallen on the aerogram. She blows on the damp spot until it is completely dry, so the pen will not leave an incriminating smudge. Even though Roma would not tell a soul, she cannot risk it. She can already hear them, the avid relatives in India who have been waiting for some‐ thing just like this to happen. *That Dutta-ginni, so set in her* ways, we knew she'd never get along with her daughter-in-law. Or worse, *Did you hear about poor Prameela, how her family treated her, yes, even her son, can you imagine?*

This much surely she owes to Sagar.

And what does she owe herself, Mrs. Dutta, falling through black night with all the certainties she trusted in collapsed upon themselves like imploded stars, and only an image inside her eyelids for company? A silhouette—man, wife, children—joined on a wall, showing her how alone she is in this land of young people. And how unnecessary.

She is not sure how long she sits under the glare of the overhead light, how long her hands clench themselves in her lap. When she opens them, nail marks line the soft flesh of her palms, red hieroglyphs—her body's language, telling her what to do.

Dear Roma, Mrs. Dutta writes,

I cannot answer your question about whether I am happy, for I am no longer sure I know what happiness is. All I know is that it isn't what I thought it to be. It isn't about being needed. It isn't about being with family either. It has something to do with love, I still think that, but in a different way than I believed earlier, a way I don't have the words to explain. Perhaps we can figure it out together, two old women drinking cha in your downstairs flat (for I do hope you will rent it to me on my return), while around us gossip falls—but lightly,

*like summer rain, for that is all we will allow it to be. If I'm lucky—
and perhaps, in spite of all that has happened, I am—the happiness
will be in the figuring out.*

Pausing to read over what she has written, Mrs. Dutta
is surprised to discover this: Now that she no longer cares
whether tears blotch her letter, she feels no need to weep.

The Intelligence
of Wild Things

THE SKY IS streaked with gray and a strange bleeding pink
I've never seen before. Or perhaps the intense cold is dis-
torting my perceptions. I huddle in a wool coat that is too
large for me, borrowed from my brother Tarun for this boat
trip, trying to remember how it feels to be warm. I am not
quite sure why we are on this ferry, why we are attempting
to cross this frozen lake whose name I cannot remember, although Tarun said it just a few minutes ago. The scratchy
wool smells—it takes me a moment to place it—of musk. It
is an odor I think of as dark and languid, the scent of the
secret, passionate body. One that I find difficult to associ-

ate with my brother, younger to me by five years, the baby of the family. How angry he would get when I called him that! And now, this smell, as new to me as the hard adult line of his jaw, dark against the blinding snowbanks of the far shore. As disturbing.

It is March in Vermont. The last day of my visit. Tomorrow I will return to Sandeep, my two daughters, my garden in Sacramento where purple bougainvilleas bloom even in winter. I haven't done what I came here to do. I haven't found a time to tell Tarun that our mother, to whom he hasn't spoken in years, is dying in India. I haven't found a way to beg him to go to her.

The *River Queen's* rusty deck shudders under my feet as the boat makes its uneven way across the lake. I can hear the crunch of ice being crushed somewhere below. Enormous metal jaws closing in underwater dimness on the huge, slippery blocks, grinding down till they crack, spraying ice needles in every direction. Perhaps there are fish down there, their slight, silver bodies mangled by the steel teeth, the water slowly turning the same pink as the sky. *Wrong again!* my brother would say if he knew what I was thinking. *The fish know to stay away from the boat. They possess the intelligence of wild things.*

Or would he? I'm not sure anymore. I pull the coat collar farther up and turn from the wind. It's been a long time since we shared our fantasies. Our fears.

I NOTICED THE photograph on his bedside stand, first thing, when I arrived from Sacramento. A laughing girl with freckled skin and reddish-gold hair. She was wearing a T-shirt and jeans which I thought of as too tight. There was a hint of blue in the background, perhaps this same lake. Even through my disapproval I noticed the maple tree she was leaning against, each green leaf perfect, webbed like amphibious fingers.

I shouldn't have been angry. I knew that. He had the right to his own life. To run around with a white girl, if that's what he wanted. He had the right not to tell me. A decade of living in this country had taught me that. Still, my face smarted as though someone had slapped it.

"Tarun, whose photo is this?"

"My girlfriend's." He spoke in English. He'd been doing that ever since I got to Vermont. It was like a mismatched dance, my long Bengali sentences, his monosyllabic, foreign answers. Was it because he had forgotten our mother tongue, or was he doing it to provoke me? Perhaps it was neither. Perhaps it was just that, after so many years among Americans, it was for him the language of least effort.

"Your girlfriend!" To my annoyance I found that I'd switched over to English, too. "You never told me you had a girlfriend, especially a white one! What is Ma going to say when she finds out!" I hated the shrill sisterly note in my voice, the banality of my response. It wasn't what I had meant to say.

Tarun shrugged. In the light of the bedside lamp, his face was as polished as an egg, as empty of guilt or concern.

"You can have the bed if you like. I'll sleep on the sofa."

For a moment, before I forced the image from my mind, I saw the girl's red hair spread over the pillow. Her pale arms tight around my brother's brown back. "No, no, it's all right," I said. "I'll be very comfortable on the sofa."

"I thought you might say that," Tarun said. The look in his eyes could have been amused, or sardonic, or merely polite.

"Are you going to let Ma know about her?" I blurted out.

It was a stupid question. Tarun hadn't written to our mother or replied to her letters ever since he came to this country. But sometimes stupidity is all we're left with.

"There's a nice movie at the Empire tonight. Want to go?"

This time I had no trouble reading my brother's eyes. They were bored.

WHAT I REMEMBER most clearly of Tarun from his child-hood are his eyes. They were very bright and very black. If

I brought my face close to his, I could see myself reflected in them, tiny and clear and more beautiful than I really was. Maybe that was why I loved him so much.

Everyone called Tarun a good boy. He never got into trouble like the other neighbor kids who talked back to teachers, or got into fistfights, or stole lozenges from the Sarada Debi All Purpose Store. Coming back from school, he rarely joined the raucous game of cricket in progress on the empty field across from our house. He preferred being with mother and me. Even when he was a teenager, he'd come into the kitchen where we were fixing dinner and knead the dough for her, or help me slice the bitter gourd. If asked, he would give us an obedient description of his day (theorems in maths class, essay test in English, atoms and molecules in science). But what he liked best was listening to my mother's stories—tales her mother had told her—of princes and princesses, wondrous talking beasts, and jewels which, touched to the walls of caverns, made secret entry-ways appear.

When they came to visit, our women relatives would compliment Ma on bringing him up so well. (They thought me too talkative, too flighty, always flipping through the foreign magazines I'd borrowed from wealthier classmates.) "And all by yourself too, a widow-woman like you," they would add, in between mouthfuls of pakoras.

"Actually, I think he's too quiet," Ma would say, frowning a little. "He spends too much time with just the two of us. I'd rather he went out and made more friends. Learned more about the world and how to feel comfortable in it. After all, I won't always be around, and his sister will soon get married and go into a different household."

"Really, Malabika!" the women would tell her, patting their mouths delicately with their handkerchiefs. "Like they say, You don't appreciate a good thing until you lose it!"

Now, with so many things slipping from my grasp, I understand the truth of that saying.

If I'd been an artist, this is what I would have painted, to keep it safe from loss—and from change, which is perhaps crueler than loss. This is what I would have brought to Tarun today: that dim kitchen, our own cave, with its safe odors of coriander and fenugreek; the small blue glow of the gas stove in the corner; three people, cross-legged on the cool cement, making food for each other while the stories wrapped us in their enchantment.

ON THE BOAT the wind yanks at my long hair, whipping it into knots that will take me hours to untangle. Across the deck from me, a group of young men in dull green parkas are joking around, jostling each other, drinking from brown paper bags. From time to time they dart sideways glances at me and my Indian clothes. I can tell they haven't seen many of us. I clutch at the boat's railings, shivering, wishing myself back in Sacramento, where no one stares when I walk to the store in my salwaar kameez. I hate it all, the knifing wind, the furtive looks, the effortless way in which my brother ignores everything equally—the cold, the men, his visiting sister. He gazes with concentration at the dead landscape as though he were alone in it. Maybe in a way he is, though in his hip-hugging jeans and army surplus jacket, he looks to me just like all the other young men on the ferry. Even the expression on his closed face is so totally *American.* This strikes me as particularly ironic. Because unlike me—who had eagerly (too eagerly?) agreed to have a marriage arranged with Sandeep mostly because he lived abroad—Tarun had never wanted to come to America.

A FEW WEEKS before Tarun arrived in Vermont, my mother wrote me a letter.

Today Taru and I had a terrible fight. He still refuses to go to college in America, although his acceptance letter has arrived. He says he wants to stay with me. But I'm terrified to keep him here. You know how bad the Naxal movement is right now in Calcutta. Every morning they find more bodies of young men in ditches. Taru keeps telling me he's safe, he doesn't belong to any political party. But that means nothing. Just last week there was a murder right on our street. Remember Supriyo, that good-looking boy? He didn't belong to any party either. I heard from Manada Pishi next door that his face was sliced to shreds. His poor mother has had a nervous breakdown. I reminded Taru of that. He still wouldn't listen.

Finally I called him a coward, hiding from the world behind his mother's sari, a fool who lived in a fantasy land. How could he throw away this opportunity, I shouted, when I'd worked so hard to bring him this far. I said he was ungrateful, a burden to me. Didn't he see that I couldn't sleep at night, worrying, because he was here? You can imagine how I hated saying it—I could see the abhimaan on his face, like a wound—but it was the only thing I knew that would make him go.

She had been right. He had gone. What she hadn't foreseen was how absolute that going would be.

Today I am thinking about the word Ma had used to describe Tarun's reaction. Abhimaan, that mix of love and anger and hurt which lies at the heart of so many of our Indian tales, and for which there is no equivalent in English. If Tarun pushed her away, would the red-haired girl feel abhimaan? Or are we capable of an emotion only when the language of our childhood has made it real in our mouths?

———

MY MOTHER'S LETTER distressed me, but it was distress of a peculiar, blurred kind. I knew how serious the situation in Calcutta was, but somehow the tragedies Ma spoke of weren't *real*, not like my own problems. The pain of my daughter's swollen gums as her first teeth came through; the smell of our apartment which, no matter how much I scrubbed, stank of stale curry; the arguments I seemed to have every evening with Sandeep and which were resolved, inevitably, the only way we knew how: by the uneasy press of our bodies against each other in bed, his mouth tasting of cloves, making me drunk, making me temporarily forget. Inescapably mundane, these things loomed so large in my world that they forced everything else to recede. A few months later, when Tarun would arrive in Vermont and call me, his voice over the phone line would be edged with a sharp, silver need. But it, too, would belong to that other plane of existence, like a flash of lightning far up in the night sky.

I hated this change in myself, this shrinking of sensibility, this failure of intelligence. But I didn't know what to do about it. Did anyone else suffer from such a disease? I was afraid to ask Sandeep, who was the only person I knew well enough in America to ask.

I kept my mother's letter for a long time at the bottom of my jewelry case, under the thick gold wedding bangles that I no longer wore because they were too elegant for my pedestrian Sacramento life. I wasn't sure if I should send it to Tarun, if that would be disloyal to my mother.

And then during a move to a new house, I lost the letter. By then it was too late, anyway.

THE FIRST FEW months after moving to this country, Tarun called me almost every day. He hated cooking for himself. Hated coming home in the evenings to an empty room. It was so cold in Vermont, he felt he was slowly freezing, one organ at a time. I forced myself to ignore the pleading in his voice. Sandeep was dead against any family— his or mine—coming to live with us. *Landing on my head* was the term he used. So I would offer Tarun a variation of We-all-went-through-the-same-thing, before-you-know-it you'll-get-used-to-this-lifestyle. It was hard to think of anything more profound to say with the baby screaming in my ear or the dal boiling over and Sandeep, like most husbands brought up in India, no help at all. Tarun would be silent for a moment. Then he would say good-bye in a quiet voice.

FOR A LONG time I didn't know about the rift between Ma and Tarun, although I wonder now whether it was more that I didn't want to know. I'd had my second baby by then, and Sandeep and I were finally falling in love. It seemed such a precarious miracle, our little house of kisses. I was afraid that even one careless word would topple it.

So when I rang up India and Ma would say that it had been a long time since she had heard from Tarun (she was too proud to say any more), could I call him and make sure he was okay, I wouldn't let myself take it seriously. *Oh, Ma!* I'd say, my gay voice drowning out her hesitant words, *Quit worrying! He isn't a baby anymore.* I'd leave a brief message on his answering machine telling him to write home, and add something cheerful about all the naughtiness his nieces had been up to. Those days, I worked hard at being cheerful because Sandeep had informed me that men disliked gloomy women.

Still, one night after Ma had been more insistent than usual, I spoke to Sandeep. I waited till after lovemaking, when he was usually in an expansive mood, and then I asked if we could have Tarun stay with us for the summer holidays.

"I'm the only family he has here, after all," I said. "And he's always been so shy, not the kind to make lots of friends—"

Sandeep touched my cheek lightly. "We're just getting to know each other. Let's give ourselves—and Tarun—a little more time alone, shall we?" When I hesitated, he sighed. "That's the trouble with our Indian families, always worrying too much. It's *good* for your brother to be on his own for a while. He's probably having a great time at the university. For all you know, he has half a dozen girlfriends and would much rather you didn't keep tabs on him."

I wanted to tell Sandeep, who was an only child, about those afternoons in Calcutta, the smell of wheat rutis browning on the skillet, the way, when Tarun entered the kitchen, a certain sternness he carried to all his day's activities fell away from his face. But Sandeep was yawning. In a moment he'd remind me that he had to get up early and go to work. I watched his lips, the way they stretched into a thin oval around his large, even teeth.

I could have argued, I know that now. I could have threatened. Sandeep needed a wife as much as I needed a husband. He feared aloneness as much as I did. But in those early days I was too unsure of myself, too much in love with being in love. It was easier to let myself believe him, to snuggle against the warm curve of his backbone and relinquish responsibility. To tell myself as I gave in to the sweet tiredness of after-sex sleep that I would have a real heart-to-heart chat with Tarun next weekend.

But something came up next weekend—and the one after, and the one after. Trips to the Laundromat, unexpected company for dinner, one of the kids running a fever. Until Tarun's phone calls became shorter and less frequent, and the pauses between his sentences were longer than all his words put together. But I wasn't listening. *Let me tell you what we did yesterday,* I'd say brightly into the silence, into the years that blurred by, while in my head I was making up the grocery list, or trying to remember when the children had to visit the dentist.

Then I came back from seeing our mother and called him to say I had to come and see him, right away, and he replied, in a carefully courteous voice so devoid of feeling that it frightened me, Sure, come if you like.

WHEN WE WERE little, Tarun and I liked to play a game called Trap the Tiger. It was played with stones and tamarind seeds—you had to encircle your opponent's stones with your seeds. All through this visit, I feel I've been playing at that game—and losing. Circling and circling Tarun with my words, their chunky, chipped syllables, only to have him slip away.

"Tarun, that was a great lasagna you fixed! When did you learn to cook so well?"

"Picked it up along the way."

"Remember when Ma used to fry us pantuas for dessert,

how we'd sit and wait for them to turn red? Remember our kitchen . . . ?"

"Mmm. Listen, do you mind if I go out for a while? I've got a couple things to take care of."

Left alone in the apartment, I would sit in front of the TV, its blank, black face. I would think of the intelligence of wild things. Geese, ants. How they knew to communicate without words, without sound. The flash of a wing, the waving of antennae. *Food. Home. This way danger lies.* I wanted to touch my fingertips to my brother's and pulse into his body all the emotions that jostled inside mine.

THE TRIP I took last month to Calcutta to see my mother was my first since I had left as a new bride, ten years ago. I was shocked by how much had changed, and how little. Caught in a traffic jam on my way from the airport to my mother's house (I was startled to discover that I no longer thought of it as mine), I had looked up at the gigantic movie billboards that towered over me. The colors were exactly as I remembered, garishly, naively brilliant. The gestures of the heroes and heroines hinted at the same exorbitant worlds of love and danger that had fascinated me as a teenager. But I didn't know a single name, and the faces on the posters were so young—so young and beautiful and hard—that I wanted to weep.

As soon as I saw her at the airport, where she had come against the doctor's advice, I knew that my mother was dying. It wasn't just the droop of her sari-blouse in a dispirited V down her thin back, or the ugly, rubber-tipped cane she leaned on, or the yellowish tint to her lips. It was the look in her eyes, the way she stared past me for a moment when I came out of the customs area, as though she didn't recognize me. As though she were looking beyond me for someone else.

I AM LEANING against the boat's railing now, looking out blindly, counting on my frozen fingers the people I love. Sandeep, my daughters, my mother, my brother. It is a pitifully short list, and does not give me the comfort I had hoped for. My mother is dying—perhaps she is already dead. How much of my husband's fondness for me is based on the convenience of give-and-take? In how many ways will my daughters and I disappoint each other as they grow from my life into their own? And my brother? I see the impatient hunch of his shoulders in army camouflage. Is he as anxious for me to be gone as I am to leave?

Swallow the icy lump that is pressing up against your throat, I order myself. Stitch a smile onto your lips. To cry now would be the final humiliation. You're going home tomorrow. You did your best, and now you're going home.

Home. I turn the sound over on my tongue, trying to figure out the various tenses in which such a word might exist. The smell of my children's damp heads after they've come in from play? Sandeep's aftershave, the way it lingered in our first bedsheets? A dim cement-floored alcove in Calcutta, the smell of frying bitter gourd, the marvel in a listening boy's eyes?

Is there ever a way back across the immigrant years, across the frozen warp of the heart?

"Look!" Tarun is pointing to a white blur on a nearby ice floe. I wipe at my eyes, hoping they haven't turned their usual telltale red, and try to show some interest. Will this miserable boat ride never end? "Look!" It's some sort of a large bird, red-beaked, with slim red legs. It isn't native to this region, judging from the comments of the parka-clad young men, but it doesn't appear to be lost. As the boat chugs closer, it spreads its white wings and looks toward us with cool self-possession. I've seen a bird like this somewhere, sometime, but I can't quite remember.

"Didi, doesn't it look like a sharash?"

Yes, indeed, it does look like the marsh crane of the Bengal countryside. But I am more startled by the Bengali name for the bird, so unexpected in my brother's mouth. That, and the childhood endearment which he hasn't used

in years. Didi. A small flash of a word, potent as any en-
chanted jewel from my mother's stories.

IT IS SOON after my father's death. I am eight, my
brother three. My harried mother, hoping for a brief re-
spite, has sent us to visit Third Uncle, out in the country.
We are homesick and miserable, suspicious of shuffly night
noises, terrified of the huge spiders studding the dark walls
of the outhouse. We do not fit in with our cousins, who
know how to milk cows and swim across the pond. We
scrape our knees when we try to climb trees with them.
They jeer if we cry.

But, today, after a morning filled with rain, the sun
glimmers around the edges of black monsoon clouds, and
the puddles are so inviting that we can't resist jumping in
them. We're muddy from head to toe, but we don't care,
even though we know Third Aunt will give us a yelling
when she sees our clothes. Defiantly, we run and run—all
the way past the rice mill, past the irrigation ditch, past the
sugarcane fields with their breathy swishing sounds. We are
running toward the rail lines. Perhaps we can jump on to a
passing train and make our way back to our mother in
Calcutta? Then abruptly we come across them, a whole
flock of sharash feeding in the flooded rice fields. My

brother lifts his delighted hands, *Look, Didi!* as the birds fly up, an arc of silver air. For a moment the sky is full of wings. Whiteness and possibility. We stand with our arms around each other until they disappear.

THE FERRY IS closer now, and everyone is looking at the bird. Even the raucous young men are quiet. The bird's eyes shine like beads of blood. It looks back at us. At me. I am sure of this. It has flown all the way from Bengal, out of the old tales, to bring me a message that will save us—if only I can hear it.

Some illusions are essential. We need them to live by.

Through a gap in the clouds the sun hangs so low over the lake that if I reached out, I could cup its burning sweetness in my palm. Lake Champlain, the name comes to me all at once. Before I returned to the States, I begged my mother to come and live with me. She refused. *I want to die in the house where your father died, where you were born, you and Taru.* Some days, the pain medication confused her.

What can I do for you, Mother? What will make you happy?

Seeing my children before I die.

But I am here, Mother.

Seeing my children before I die. Seeing my children . . .

All of us groping in caverns, our fingertips raw against

stone, searching for that slight crack, the edge of a door opening into love.

Suddenly I am glad about the girl with the red-gold hair.

The bird takes off, beating its powerful wings, wheeling with confident grace over our heads. I'm certain that my brother doesn't remember that long-ago day in the countryside. Still, I step closer. Touch the sleeve of his jacket. He looks as though he might move away. Then he puts his arm around my shoulders and gives them a brief, awkward hug.

Tonight I will tell my brother a story. *Once there was a widow-woman who had two children.* I'll tell it the way the old tales were told, without guilt or blame, out of sorrow and hope, in honor of memory. Maybe he won't listen, and maybe he will.

We stand side by side, shoulders touching. The wind blows through us, a wild, intelligent wind. The white bird flies directly into the sun.

THE LIVES OF STRANGERS

THE SEEPAGE OF rainwater has formed a tapestry against the peeling walls of the Nataraj Yatri House dining hall, but no one except Leela notices this. The other members of the pilgrimage party jostle around the fire that sputters in a corner and shout at the pahari boy to hurry with the tea. Aunt Seema sits at one of the scratched wooden tables with a group of women, all of them swaddled in the bright shawls they bought for this trip. From time to time they look down at their laps with a startled expression, like sparrows who have awakened to find themselves plumaged in cockatoo feathers.

Aunt beckons to Leela to come sit by her. "Baap re," she says, "I can't believe how cold it is here in Kashmir. It's quite delightful, actually. Just think, in Calcutta right now people are bathing in sweat, even with the fans on full speed!"

The women smile, pleased at having had the foresight to leave sweaty Calcutta behind at the height of summer for a journey which is going to earn them comfort on earth and goodwill in heaven. They hold their chins high and elongate their necks as classical dancers might. Plump, middle-aged women who sleepily read love stories in *Desh* magazine through the interminable train journey from Howrah Station, already they are metamorphosed into handmaidens of Shiva, adventure-bound toward his holy shrine in Amarnath. Their eyes sparkle with zeal as they discuss how remote the shrine is. How they will have to walk across treacherous glaciers for three whole days to reach it. Contemplating them, Leela wonders if this is the true lure of travel, this hope of a transformed self. Will her own journey, begun when she left America a month ago, bring her this coveted change?

Tea arrives, sweet and steaming in huge aluminum kettles, along with dinner: buttery wheat parathas, fatly stuffed with spicy potatoes. When they have eaten, the guide advises them to get their rest. This is no touristy excursion, he reminds them sternly. It is a serious and sacred yatra, and dangerous, too. He talks awhile of the laws to be observed while on pilgrimage: no non-vegetarian food, no sex. Any menstruating women should not proceed beyond this point. There is a lot more, but his Bengali is full of long, formal words that Leela does not know, and her attention wanders. He ends by saying something about sin and expiation, which seems to her terribly complex and thus very Indian.

Later in bed, Leela will think of Mrs. Das. At dinner Mrs. Das sat by herself at a table that was more rickety than the others. In a room filled with nervous laughter (for the headman had frightened them all a bit, though no one would admit it) she held herself with an absorbed stillness, her elbows pulled close as though early in life she had been taught not to take up too much space in the world. She did not speak to anyone. Under her frizzy pepper-colored hair, her face was angular and ascetic.

Leela has not met Mrs. Das, but she knows a great deal about her because Aunt Seema's friends discuss her frequently. Mostly they marvel at her bad luck.

"Can you imagine!" the doctor's wife says. "Her husband died just two years after her marriage, and right away her in-laws, who hated her because it had been a love match, claimed that the marriage wasn't legal. They were filthy rich—the Dases of Tollygunge, you understand—they hired the shrewdest lawyers. She lost everything—the money, the house, even the wedding jewelry."

"No justice in this world," Aunt says, clicking her tongue sympathetically.

"She had to go to work in an office," someone else adds. "Think of it, a woman of good family, forced to work with low-caste peons and clerks! That's how she put her son through college and got him married."

"And now the daughter-in-law refuses to live with her," Aunt says. "So she's had to move into a women's hostel. A women's hostel! At her age!"

The doctor's wife shakes her head mournfully. "Some people are like that, born under an unlucky star. They bring bad luck to themselves and everyone close to them."

Leela studies the kaleidoscope of emotions flitting across the women's faces. Excitement, pity, cheerful outrage. Can it be true, that part about an unlucky star? In America she would have dealt with such superstition with fluent, dismissive ease, but India is complicated. Like entering a murky, primal lake, in India she has to watch her step.

LEELA'S HAPPIEST CHILDHOOD memories were of aloneness: reading in her room with the door closed, playing chess on the computer, embarking on long bike rides through the city, going to the movies by herself. You saw more that way, she explained to her parents. You didn't miss crucial bits of dialogue because your companion was busy making inane remarks. Her parents, themselves solitary individuals, didn't object. People—except for a selected handful—were noisy and messy. They knew that. Which was why, early in their lives, they had escaped India to take up research positions in America. Ever since Leela could remember, they had encouraged her taste for privacy. When Leela became a computer programmer, they applauded the fact that she could do most of her work from home. When she became involved with Dexter, another programmer whom she had met at one of the rare conferences she attended, they applauded that too, though more cautiously.

Her relationship with Dexter was a brief affair, perhaps inevitably so. Looking back in search of incidents to remember it by, Leela would only be able to recall a general feeling, something like being wound tightly in a blanket on a cold day, comforting yet restrictive. Even when things were at their best, they never moved in together. Leela preferred it that way. She preferred, too, to sleep alone, and often moved after lovemaking to the spare bed in her apartment. When you slept, you were too vulnerable. Another person's essence could invade you. She had explained it once to Dexter. He had stroked her hair with fingers she thought of as sensitive and artistic, and had seemed to understand. But apparently he hadn't. It was one of the facts he dwelt on at some bitter length before he left.

"You're like one of those spiny creatures that live at the bottom of the ocean," he said. "Everything just slides off of that watertight shell of yours. You don't need me—you don't need *anyone*."

He wasn't totally right about that. A week after he left, Leela ended up in the emergency ward, having swallowed a bottle of sleeping pills.

An encounter with death—even an aborted one (Leela had called 911 as soon as she finished taking the pills)—alters one in unaccountable ways. After having to deal with the hospital, the police, and the mandatory counselor assigned to her, Leela should have heaved a sigh of relief when she returned to her quiet, tidy apartment. Instead, for the first time, she found her own company inadequate. Alone, there seemed no point in opening the drapes or cleaning up the TV dinner containers stacked up on the coffee table. The place took on a green, underwater dimness. Her computer gathered dust as she wandered from room to room, sometimes with her eyes closed, trailing her fingers as though they were fins across the furniture, testing the truth of Dexter's accusation.

She didn't know when it was that she started thinking

about India, which she had never visited. The idea attached itself to the underneath of her mind and grew like a barnacle. In her imagination the country was vast and vague. Talismanic. For some reason she associated it with rain, scavenger crows, the clanging of orange trams, and the purplish-green of elephant-ears. Were these items from some story her parents had told in her childhood? No. Though her parents' stories had spanned many topics—from the lives of famous scientists to the legends of Greece and Rome— they never discussed their homeland, a country they seemed to have shed as easily and completely as a lizard drops its tail.

When she called her parents to inform them she was going, she did not tell them why. Perhaps she herself did not know. Nor did she speak of the suicide attempt, which filled her with a rush of mortification whenever it intruded on her thoughts. As always with her decisions, they did not venture advice, though she thought she heard her mother suppress a sigh. They waited to see if she had more to say, and when she didn't, they told her how to contact Aunt Seema, who was her mother's cousin.

"Try to stay away from the crowds," her father said.

"That's impossible," said her mother. "Just be sure to take your shots before you go, drink boiled water at all times, and don't get involved in the lives of strangers."

WHAT DID LEELA expect from India? The banalities of heat and dust, poverty and squalor, yes. The elated confusion of city streets where the beetle-black Ambassador cars of the rich inched their way, honking, between sweating rickshaw-pullers and cows who stood unmoving, as dignified as dowagers. But she had not thought Calcutta would vanquish her so easily with its melancholy poetry of old cotton saris hung out to dry on rooftops. With low-ceilinged groceries filled with odors she did not recognize but knew to be indispensable. In the evenings, the shopkeeper waved a lamp in front of a vividly colored calendar depicting Rama's coronation. His waiting customers did not seem to mind. Sometimes at dawn she stood at her bedroom window and heard, cutting through the roar of buses, the cool, astonishing voice of a young man in a neighboring house practicing a morning raag.

At the airport, Aunt Seema had been large, untidy, and moist—the exact opposite of Leela's mother. She launched herself at Leela with a delighted cry, kissing her on both cheeks, pulling her into her ample, talcum-powder-scented bosom, exclaiming how overjoyed she was to meet her. In America Leela would have been repelled by such effusion, especially from a woman she had never seen in her life. Here it seemed as right—and as welcome—as the too-sweet glass of orange squash that the maid brought her as soon as she reached the house.

Aunt dressed Leela in her starched cotton saris, put matching bindis on her forehead, and lined her eyes with kajal. She forced her to increase her rudimentary Bengali vocabulary by refusing to speak to her in English. She cooked her rui fish sautéed with black jeera, and moglai parathas stuffed with eggs and onions, which had to be flipped over deftly at a crucial moment—food Leela loved, though it gave her heartburn. She took her to the Kalighat temple for a blessing, to night-long music concerts, and to the homes of her friends, all of whom wanted to arrange a marriage for her. Leela went unprotestingly. Like a child acting in her first play, she was thrilled by the vibrant unreality of the life she was living. At night she lay in the big bed beside Aunt (Uncle having been banished to a cot downstairs) and watched the soft white swaying of the mosquito net in the breeze from the ceiling fan. She pondered the unexpected pleasure she took in every disorganized aspect of the day. India was a Mardi Gras that never ended. Who would have thought she'd feel so at home here?

So when Aunt Seema said, "You want to see the real India, the spiritual India? Let's go on a pilgrimage," she agreed without hesitation.

THE TALK STARTS at the end of the first day's trek. In one of the women's tents, where Leela lies among pilgrims who huddle in blankets and nurse aching muscles, a voice rises from the dark.

"Do you know, Mrs. Das's bedroll didn't get to the camp. They can't figure out what happened—the guides swear they tied it onto a mule this morning. . . ."

"That's right," responds another voice. "I heard them complaining because they had to scrounge around in their own packs to find her some blankets."

In the anonymous darkness, the voices take on cruel, choric tones. They release suspicion into the close air like bacteria, ready to multiply wherever they touch down.

"It's like that time on the train, remember, when she was the only one who got food poisoning. . . ."

"Yes, yes . . ."

"I wonder what will happen next. . . ."

"As long as it doesn't affect us. . . ."

"How can you be sure? Maybe next time it will. . . ."

"I hate to be selfish, but I wish she wasn't here with us at all. . . ."

"Me, too . . ."

Leela wonders about the tent in which Mrs. Das is spending her night. She wonders what people are saying in there. What they are thinking. An image comes to her with a brief, harsh clarity: the older woman's body curled into a lean comma under her borrowed blankets. In the whispery dark, her thin, veined lids squeezed shut in a semblance of sleep.

STRUGGLING UP THE trail through the morning mist, the line of pilgrims in gay woolen clothes looks like a bright garland. Soon the light will grow brutal and blinding, but at this hour it is sleepy, diffuse. A woman pauses to chant. *Om Namah Shivaya, Salutations to the Auspicious One.* The notes tremble in the air, Leela thinks, like silver bubbles. The pilgrims are quiet—there's something about the snowy crags that discourages gossip. The head guide has suggested that walking time be utilized for reflection and repentance. Leela finds herself thinking, instead, of accidents.

She remembers the first one most clearly. It must have been a special occasion, maybe a birthday or an out-of-town visitor, because her mother was cooking. She rarely made Indian food from scratch, and Leela remembers that she was snappish and distracted. Wanting to help, the four-year-old Leela had pulled at a pot and seen the steaming dal come at her in a yellow rush. It struck her arm with a slapping sound. She screamed and raced around the kitchen—as though agony could be outrun. Long after her mother immersed her arm in ice water and gave her Tylenol to reduce the pain, she continued to sob—tears of rage at being tricked, Leela realizes now. She'd had no intimations, until then, that good intentions were no match for the forces of the physical world.

More accidents followed, in spite of the fact that she was not a particularly physical child. They blur together in Leela's memory like the landscape outside a speeding car's windows. She fell from her bike in front of a moving car— luckily the driver had good reflexes, and she only needed a few stitches on her chin. She sat in the passenger seat of her mother's van, and a stone—from who knows where— shattered the windshield, filling Leela's lap with jagged silver. A defective electrical wire caught fire at night in her bedroom while she slept. Her mother, up for a drink of water, smelled the smoke and ran to the bedroom to discover the carpet smoldering around the sleeping Leela's bed. Do all these close escapes mean that Leela is lucky? Or is her unlucky star, thwarted all this time by some imbalance in the stratosphere, waiting for its opportunity?

She thinks finally of the suicide attempt which, since she arrived in India, she has quarantined in a part of her mind she seldom visits. Can it be classified as an accident, an accident she did to herself? She remembers the magnetic red gleam of the round pills in the hollow of her palm, how unexpectedly solid they had felt, like metal pellets. The shriek of the ambulance outside her window. The old man who lived across the hall peering from a crack in his door, grim and unsurprised. The acidic ache in her throat when they pumped her stomach. Leela had kept her eyes on the wall of the emergency room afterward, too ashamed to look at the paramedic who was telling her something. Something cautionary and crucial which might help her now, as she steps warily along this beautiful glacial trail, watching for crevasses. But for her life she cannot recall what it was.

EACH NIGHT THE pilgrims are assigned to different tents by the head guide, according to some complicated logic Leela has failed to decipher. But tonight, when she finds herself in Mrs. Das's tent, her bedroll set down next to the older woman's makeshift one, she wonders if it is destiny that has brought her here.

All her life, like her parents, Leela has been a believer in individual responsibility. But lately she finds herself wondering. When she asked Aunt Seema yesterday, she touched Leela's cheek in a gesture of amused affection. "Ah, my dear—to believe that you control everything in your life! How absurdly American!"

Destiny is a seductive concept. Ruminating on it, Leela

feels the events of her life turn weightless and pass through her like clouds. The simplistic, sublunary words she assigned to them—*pride, shame, guilt, folly*—no longer seem to apply.

"Please," Mrs. Das whispers in Bengali, startling Leela from thought. She sits on the tarpaulin floor of the tent, propped against her bedroll, her legs splayed out crookedly from under her sari. "Could you ask one of the attendants to bring some warm water? My feet hurt a lot."

"Of course," Leela says, jumping up. An odd gladness fills her as she performs this small service. Aunt, who was less than happy about Leela's tent assignment tonight, had whispered to her to be sure to stay away from Mrs. Das. But Aunt is at the other end of the camp, while destiny has placed Leela here.

When the water comes in a bucket, Mrs. Das surreptitiously removes her shoes. They are made of rough leather, cheap and unlovely. They make Leela feel guilty about her fleece-lined American boots, even though the fleece is fake. Then she sucks in a horrified breath.

Freed of shoes and socks, Mrs. Das's feet are in bad shape, swollen all the way to the calves. The toes are blistered and bluish with frostbite. The heels weep yellowish pus. Mrs. Das looks concerned but not surprised—this has obviously been going on for a couple of days. She grits her teeth, lurches to her feet, and tries to lift the bucket. Leela takes it from her and follows her to the opening of the tent, and when Mrs. Das has difficulty bending over to wash her feet, she kneels and does it for her. She feels no disgust as she cleans off the odorous pus. This intrigues her. Usually she doesn't like touching people. Even with her parents, she seldom went beyond the light press of lips to cheek, the hurried pat on the shoulder. In her Dexter days, if he put his arm around her, she'd find an excuse to move away after a few minutes. Yet here she is, tearing strips from an old sari and bandaging Mrs. Das's feet, her fingers moving with a deft intelligence she did not suspect they possessed, brown against the matching brown of Mrs. Das's skin. This is the first time, she thinks, that she has known such intimacy. How amazing that it should be a stranger who has opened her like a dictionary and brought to light this word whose definition had escaped her until now.

SOMEONE IN THE tent must have talked, for here through the night comes the party's doctor, his flashlight making a ragged circle of brightness on the tent floor as he enters. "Now what's the problem?" he asks Mrs. Das, who attempts a look of innocence. What problem could he be referring to? The doctor sighs, hands Leela his torch, re-

moves the sari strips, and clicks his tongue gravely as he examines Mrs. Das's feet. There's evidence of infection, he
says. She needs a tetanus shot immediately, and even then
the blisters might get septic. How could she have been so
foolish as to keep this a secret from him? He pulls a thick
syringe from his bag and administers an injection. "But you
still have to get down to the hospital at Pahelgaon as soon
as possible," he ends. "I'll ask the guide to find some way
of sending you back tomorrow."

Mrs. Das clutches the doctor's arm. In the flashlight's
erratic beam, her eyes, magnified behind thick glasses, glint
desperately. She doesn't care about her feet, she says. It's
more important for her to complete the pilgrimage—she's
waited so long to do it. They're only a day or so away from
Shiva's shrine. If she had to turn back now, it would kill
her much more surely than a septic blister.

The doctor's walrus mustache droops unhappily. He
takes a deep breath and says that two extra days of hard
walking could cause gangrene to set in, though a brief un-
certainty flits over his face as he speaks. He repeats that
Mrs. Das must go back tomorrow, then hurries off before
she can plead further.

The darkness left behind is streaked with faint cobwebs
of moonlight. Leela glances at the body prone on the bedding next to her. Mrs. Das is completely quiet, and this

frightens Leela more than any fit of hysterics. She hears shufflings from the other end of the tent, whispered comments sibilant with relief. Angrily, she thinks that had the patient been anyone else, the doctor would not have been so adamant about sending her back. The moon goes behind a cloud; around her, darkness packs itself tightly, like black wool. She pushes her hand through it to where she thinks Mrs. Das's arm might be. Against her fingers Mrs. Das's skin feels brittle and stiff, like cheap waterproof fabric. Leela holds Mrs. Das's wrist awkwardly, not knowing what to do. In the context of Indian etiquette, would patting be considered a condescending gesture? She regrets her impetuosity.

Then Mrs. Das turns her wrist—it is the swift movement of a night animal who knows its survival depends on mastering such economies of action—and clasps Leela's fingers tightly in her own.

LATE THAT NIGHT, Mrs. Das tries to continue up the trail on her own, is spotted by the lookout guide, apprehended and brought back. It happens quickly and quietly, and Leela sleeps through it all.

By the time she wakes, the tent is washed in calm mountain light and abuzz with women and gossip.

"There she was, in the dark on her own, without any supplies, not even an electric torch, can you imagine?"

"Luckily the guide saw her before she went beyond the bend in the mountain. Otherwise she'd be in a ravine by now. . . ."

"Or frozen to death . . ."

"Crazy woman! They say when they caught her, she fought them tooth and nail—I'm telling you, she actually drew blood! Like someone possessed by an evil spirit."

Leela stares at Mrs. Das's bedroll, two dark, hairy blankets topped by a sheet. It looks like the peeled skin of an animal turned inside out. The women's excitement crackles through the air, sends little shocks up her arms. Are people in India harder to understand because they've had so many extra centuries to formulate their beliefs? She recalls the expression on Dexter's face before he slammed the door, the simple incandescence of his anger. In some way, she had expected it all along. But Mrs. Das . . . ? She curls her fingers, remembering the way the older woman had clasped them in her dry, birdlike grip.

"Did she really think she could get to the shrine all by herself!" someone exclaims.

Leela spots Aunt Seema and tugs at her sari. "Where is Mrs. Das now?"

"The guides have put her in a separate tent where they

can keep an eye on her until they can send her back," Aunt says, shaking her head sadly. "Poor thing—I really feel sorry for her. Still, I must confess I'm glad she's leaving." Then a suspicious frown takes over her face. "Why do you want to know? Did you talk to her last night? Leela, stop, where are you going?"

MRS. DAS, WHOM Leela finds in a small tent outside which a guide keeps watch, does not look like a woman who has recently battled several men tooth and nail. Cowled in a faded green shawl, she dozes peacefully against the tent pole, though this could be due to the Calmpose tablets the doctor has made her take. Or perhaps there's not much outside her head that she's interested in at this point. She has lost her glasses in her night's adventuring, and when Leela touches her shoulder, she looks up, blinking with dignity.

Leela opens her mouth to say she is sorry about how Mrs. Das has been treated. But she hears herself saying, "I'm going back with you." The dazed expression on Mrs. Das's face mirrors her own inner state. When after a moment Mrs. Das warily asks her why, all she can do is shrug her shoulders. She is uncertain of her motives. Is it her desire to prove (but to whom?) that she is somehow superior to the others? Is it pity, an emotion she has always distrusted? Is it some inchoate affinity she feels toward this stranger? But if you believe in destiny, no one can be a stranger, can they? There's always a connection, a reason because of which people enter your orbit, bristling with dark energy like a meteor intent on collision.

TRAVELING DOWN A mountain trail fringed by fat, seeded grasses the same gray as the sky, Leela wants to ask Mrs. Das about destiny. Whether she believes in it, what she understands it to encompass. But Mrs. Das grips the saddle of the mule she is sitting on, her body rigid with the single-minded terror of a person who has never ridden an animal. Ahead, the guide's young, scraggly-bearded son whistles a movie tune Leela remembers having heard in another world, during an excursion with Aunt Seema to some Calcutta market.

Aunt Seema was terribly upset with Leela's decision to accompany Mrs. Das—no, even with that intense adverb, *upset* is too simple a word to describe the change in her urbane aunt, who had taken such gay control of Leela's life in the city. The new Aunt Seema wrung her hands and lamented, "But what would your mother say if she knew that I let you go off alone with some stranger?" (Did she really believe Leela's mother would hold her responsible?

The thought made Leela smile.) Aunt's face was full of awful conviction as she begged Leela to reconsider. Breaking off a pilgrimage like this, for no good reason, would rouse the wrath of Shiva. When Leela said that the occurrences of her life were surely of no interest to a deity, Aunt gripped her shoulders with trembling hands.

"Stop!" she cried, her nostrils flaring. "You don't know what you're saying! That bad-luck woman, she's bewitched you!"

How many unguessed layers there were to people, skins that came loose at an unexpected tug, revealing raw, fearful flesh. Amazing, that folks could love one another in the face of such unreliability! It made Leela at once sad and hopeful.

WALKING DOWNHILL, LEELA has drifted into a fantasy. In it, she lives in a small rooftop flat on the outskirts of Calcutta. Mrs. Das, whom she has rescued from the women's hostel, lives with her. They have a maid who shops and runs their errands, so the women rarely need to leave the flat. Each evening they sit on the terrace beside the potted roses and chrysanthemums (Mrs. Das has turned out to be a skillful gardener) and listen to music—a tape of Bengali folk songs (Mrs. Das looks like a person who would enjoy that), or maybe one of Leela's jazz CDs to which Mrs. Das listens with bemused attention. When they wish each other good night, she touches Leela's arm. "Thank you," she says, her eyes deep as a forest.

They have come to a riverbed. There isn't much water, but the boulders on which they step are slippery with moss. It's starting to rain, and the guide eyes the sky nervously. He pulls at the balking mule, which stumbles. Mrs. Das gives a harsh, crowlike cry and flings out her hand. Leela grasps it and holds on until they reach the other side.

"Thank you," says Mrs. Das. It is the first time she has smiled, and Leela sees that her eyes are, indeed, deep as a forest.

"BUT, MADAM!" THE proprietor at the Nataraja inn cries to Leela in an English made shaky by distress. "You people are not to be coming back for two more days! Already I am giving your rooms to other pilgrim party. Whole hotel is full. This is middle of pilgrim season—other hotels are also being full." He gives Leela and Mrs. Das, who are shivering in their wet clothes, an accusing look. "How is it you two are returned so soon?"

The guide, who has brought in the bedrolls, says something in a rapid Pahari dialect that Leela cannot follow. The clerk pulls back his head in a swift, turtlelike motion and gives Mrs. Das a glance full of misgiving.

"Please," Leela says. "We're very tired, and it's raining. Can't you find us something?"

"Sorry, madams. Maybe Mughal Gardens in market-place is having space. . . ."

Leela can feel Mrs. Das's placid eyes on her. It is obvious that she trusts the younger woman to handle the situation. Leela sighs. Being a savior in real life has drawbacks she never imagined in her rooftop fantasy. Recalling something Aunt Seema said earlier, she digs in the waistband of her sari and comes up with a handful of rupee notes which she lays on the counter.

The clerk rocks back on his heels, torn between avarice and superstition. Then his hand darts out and covers the notes. "We are having a small-small storeroom on top of hotel. Big enough for one person only." He parts his lips in an ingenuous smile. "Maybe older madam can try Mughal Gardens?"

Leela gives him a reprimanding look. "We'll manage," she says.

THE CLERK HAS not exaggerated. The room, filled with discarded furniture, is about as big as Leela's queen-size bed in America. Even after the sweeper carries all the junk out into the corridor, there isn't enough space to open the two bedrolls without their edges overlapping. Leela tries to hide her dismay. It strikes her that since she arrived in India, she has not been alone even once. With sudden homesickness, she longs for her wide, flat bedroom, its uncomplicated vanilla walls, its window from which she had looked out on to nothing more demanding than a clump of geraniums.

"I've caused you a lot of inconvenience."

Mrs. Das's voice is small but not apologetic. (Leela rather likes this.) "You shouldn't have come back with me," she adds matter-of-factly. "What if I *am* bad luck, like people believe?"

"Do you believe that?" Leela asks. She strains to hear Mrs. Das's answer above the crash of thunder.

"Belief, disbelief." Mrs. Das shrugs. "So many things I believed to be one way turned out otherwise. I believed my son's marriage wouldn't change things between us. I believed I would get to Shiva's shrine, and all my problems would disappear. Last night on the mountain I believed the best thing for me would be to fall into a crevasse and die." She smiles with unexpected sweetness as she says this. "But now—here we are together."

Together. When Mrs. Das says it in Bengali, *eksangay*, the word opens inside Leela with a faint, ringing sound, like a distant temple bell.

"I have something I want to give you," Mrs. Das says.

"No, no," says Leela, embarrassed. "Please, I'd rather you didn't."

"He who gives," says Mrs. Das, "must be prepared to receive." Is this an ancient Indian saying, or one that she has made up herself? And what exactly does it mean? Is giving then a privilege, in return for which you must allow others the opportunity to do the same? Mrs. Das unclasps a thin gold chain she is wearing. She leans forward and Leela feels her fingers fumbling for a moment on the nape of her neck. She wants to protest, to explain to Mrs. Das that she has always hated jewelry, all that metal clamped around you. But she is caught in a web of unfamiliar ideas. Is giving the touchstone by which the lives of strangers become your own? The expression on Mrs. Das's face is secretive, prayerful. And then the skin-warm, almost weightless chain is around Leela's throat.

Mrs. Das switches off the naked bulb that hangs on a bit of wire from the ceiling. The two of them lie down, each on her blanket, and listen to the wind, which moans and rattles the shutters like a madwoman wanting to be let in. Leela hopes Aunt Seema is safe, that the storm has not hit the mountain the way it has Pahelgaon. But the world outside this square, contained room has receded so far that she is unable to feel anxiety. Rain falls all around her, insulating as a lullaby. If she were to stretch out her arm, she would touch Mrs. Das's face.

She says, softly, "Once I tried to kill myself."

Mrs. Das says nothing. Perhaps she is asleep.

Leela finds herself speaking of the pills, the ambulance, the scraped-out space inside her afterward. Perhaps it had always been there, and she had not known? She talks about her father and mother, their unbearable courtesy, which she sees only this moment as having been unbearable. She asks questions about togetherness, about being alone. What the value of each might be. She sends her words into the night, and does not need a reply.

She has never spoken so much in her life. In the middle of a sentence, she falls asleep.

LEELA IS DREAMING. In the dream, the glacial trails have been washed away by rain. She takes a false step, sinks into slush. Ice presses against her chest. She opens her mouth to cry for help, and it, too, fills with ice. With a thunderous crack, blackness opens above her, a brilliant and brutal absence of light. She knows it has found her finally, her unlucky star.

Leela wakes, her heart clenched painfully like an arthritic fist. How real the dream was. Even now she feels the freezing weight on her chest, hears the ricochet of the cracked-open sky. But, no, it is not just a dream. Her blanket is soaked through, and the floor is awash with water. She scrabbles for the light switch and sees, in the dim glare, a corner of the roof hanging down, swinging drunkenly. In the midst of all this, Mrs. Das sleeps on, covers pulled over her head. Leela is visited by a crazy wish to lie down beside her.

"Quick, quick!" she cries, shaking her. "We have to get out of here before that roof comes down."

Mrs. Das doesn't seem to understand what Leela wants from her. Another gust of wind hits the roof, which gives an ominous creak. Her eyes widen, but she makes no move to sit up.

"Come on," shouts Leela. She starts to drag her to the door. Mrs. Das offers neither resistance nor help. A long time back Leela had taken a CPR course, she has forgotten why. Mrs. Das's body, slack and rubbery, reminds her of the dummy on whose chest she had pounded with earnest energy. The thought depresses her, and this depression is the last emotion she registers before something hits her head.

LEELA LIES ON a lumpy mattress. Even with her eyes closed, she knows that the clothes she is wearing—a baggy blouse, a limp cotton sari which swathes her loosely—are not hers. Her head feels stuffed with steel shavings. Is she in heaven, having died a heroic death? But surely celestial bedding would be more comfortable, celestial clothing more elegant—even in India? She is ashamed of having thought that last phrase. She moves her head a little. The jab of pain is like disappointed lightning.

"Doctor, doctor, she's waking up," Aunt Seema says from somewhere, her voice damp and wobbly like a cracker that's been dunked in tea. But why is Leela thinking like this? She knows she should appreciate her aunt's loving concern and say something to reassure her. But it is so private, so comfortable, behind her closed eyes.

"Finally," says the doctor's voice. "I was getting worried." Leela can smell his breath—it's cigarettes, a brand she does not know. It smells of cloves. When she has forgotten everything else, she thinks, she will remember the odors of this journey.

"Can you hear me, Leela?" the doctor asks. "Can you open your eyes?" He taps on her cheek with maddening persistence until she gives up and glares at him.

"You're lucky, young lady," he says as he changes the bandage around her head. "You should be thankful you were hit by a piece of wood. Now if that had been a sheet of rusted metal—"

Lucky. Thankful. Leela doesn't trust such words. They change their meaning as they swoop, sharp-clawed, about her head. The room is full of women; they wring their hands in gestures that echo her aunt's. She closes her eyes again. There's a question she must ask, an important one—but when she tries to catch it in a net of words, it dissolves into red fog.

"It's all my fault," Aunt Seema says in a broken voice that baffles Leela. Why should Aunt feel so much distress at problems which are, after all, hers alone? "Leela doesn't understand these things—how can she?—but I should have made her stay away from that accursed woman. . . ."

"Do try to be quiet." The doctor's voice is testy, as though he has heard this lament many times already. "Give her the medicine and let her rest."

Someone holds Leela's head, brings a cup to her lips. The medicine is thick and vile. She forces it down her throat with harsh satisfaction. Aunt sobs softly, in deference to the doctor's orders. Her friends murmur consolations. From time to time, phrases rise like a refrain from their crooning: *The poor girl, Shiva have mercy, that bad-luck woman, oh, what will I tell your mother.*

A commotion at the door.

"I've got to see her, just for a minute, just to make sure she's all right—"

There's a heaving inside Leela.

"No," says one of the women. "Daktar-babu said, no excitement."

"Please, I won't talk to her—I'll just take a look."

"Over my dead body you will," Aunt Seema bursts out. "Haven't you done her enough harm already? Go away. Leela, you tell her yourself . . ."

Leela doesn't want to tell anyone anything. She wants only to sleep. Is that too much to ask for? A line comes to her from a poem, *Death's second self which seals up all in rest.* She imagines snow, great fluffy quilts of it, packed around her. But the voices scrape at her, *Leela, Leela, Leela.*

The room is full of evening. Leela sees Mrs. Das at the door, trying to push her way past the determined bulk of the doctor's wife. Her disheveled hair radiates from her head like crinkly white wires, giving her, for a moment, the look of an alien in a *Star Trek* movie. When she sees that Leela's eyes are open, she stops struggling and reaches out toward her.

Why does Leela do what she does next? Is it the medication, which makes her light-headed? The pain, which won't let her think? Or is it some dark, genetic strain which, unknown to her, has pierced her pragmatic American upbringing with its sharp, knotted root? At times, later, she will tell herself, *I didn't know what I was doing.* At other times, she'll say, *Liar.* For doesn't her response to Mrs. Das come from the intrinsic and fearful depths of who she is? The part of her that knows she is no savior?

Leela sits up in bed. "Aunt's right," she says. Her teeth

chatter as though she is fevered. "All of them are right. You *are* cursed. Go away. Leave me alone."

"No," says Mrs. Das. But it is a pale sound, without conviction.

"Yes!" says Leela. "Yes!" She grasps the chain Mrs. Das has given her and yanks at it. The worn gold gives easily. Falling, it makes a small, skittery sound on the wood floor.

Darkness is bursting open around Leela like black chrysanthemums.

Mrs. Das stares at the chain, then turns and stumbles from the room. Her shadow, long and misshapen, touches Leela once. Then it, too, is gone.

THE PILGRIMAGE PARTY makes much of Leela as she lies recovering. The women bring her little gifts from their forays into town—an embroidered purse, a bunch of Kashmiri grapes, a lacquered jewelry box. When they hold out the presents, Leela burrows her hands into her blanket. But the women merely nod to each other. They whisper words like *shock* and *been through so much*. They hand the gifts to Aunt, who promises to keep them safely until Leela is better. When they leave, she feels like a petulant child.

From the doorway, the men ask Aunt Seema how Leela is coming along. Their voices are gruff and hushed, their eyes furtive with awe—as though she were a martyr-saint who took upon herself the bad luck that would have otherwise fallen on them. Is it cynical to think this? There is no one any more whom Leela can ask.

ON THE WAY back to Srinagar, where the party will catch the train to Calcutta, by unspoken consent Leela is given the best seat on the bus, up front near the big double windows.

"It's a fine view, and it won't joggle you so much," says one of the women, plumping up a pillow for her. Another places a foot rest near her legs. Aunt Seema unscrews a Thermos and pours her a glass of pomegranate juice—to replace all the blood Leela lost, she says. The juice is the color of blood. Its thin tartness makes Leela's mouth pucker up, and Aunt says, in a disappointed voice, "Oh, dear, is it not so sweet then? Why, that Bahadur at the hotel swore to me . . ."

Leela feels ungracious, boorish. She feels angry for feeling this way. "I have a headache," she says and turns to the window where, hidden behind her sunglasses, she watches the rest of the party get on the bus. Amid shouts and laughter, the bus begins to move.

She waits until the bus has lurched its way around three

hairpin bends. Then she says, "Aunt...?" She tries to make her voice casual, but the words come out in a croak.

"Yes, dear? A little more juice?" Aunt asks hopefully.

"Where is Mrs. Das? Why didn't she get on the bus?"

Aunt fiddles with the catch of her purse. Her face indicates her discomfort at the baldness of Leela's questions. A real Indian woman would have known to approach the matter delicately, sideways.

But the doctor's wife, who is sitting behind them, leans forward to say, "Oh, her! She went off somewhere on her own, when was it, three, no, four nights ago, right after she created that ruckus in your sickroom. She didn't take her bedroll with her, or even her suitcase. Strange, no? Personally, I think she's a little bit touched up here." She taps her head emphatically.

Misery swirls, acidic, through Leela's insides. She raises her hand with great effort to cover her mouth, so it will not spill out.

"Are you okay, dear?" Aunt asks.

"She looks terribly pale," the doctor's wife says. "It's all these winding roads—enough to make anyone vomity."

"I might have some lemon drops," says Aunt, rummaging in her handbag.

Leela accepts the sour candy and turns again to the window. Behind her she hears the doctor's wife's carrying whisper: "If I were you, I'd get a puja done for your niece once you get to Calcutta. You know, to avert the evil eye . . ."

Outside the bus, mountains and waterfalls are speeding past Leela. Sunlight slides like opportunity from the narrow green leaves of debdaru trees and is lost in the underbrush. What had the guide said, at the start of the trip, about expiation? Leela cannot remember. And even if she did, would she be capable of executing those gestures, delicate and filled with power, like the movements of a Bharatnatyam dancer, which connect humans to the gods and to each other? Back in America, her life waits to claim her, unchanged, impervious, smelling like floor polish. In the dusty window, her reflection is a blank oval. She takes off her dark glasses to see better, but the features which peer back at her are unfamiliar, as though they belong to someone she has never met.

The Love of a Good Man

WHEN I WAS growing up in Calcutta, my mother had a saying she was fond of: *The love of a good man can save your life.*

It's not an exclusively Indian sentiment. Here in San Jose, California, too, I've heard women saying the same thing, even women I admire. But somehow, whenever I heard it, the voice would be overlaid with my mother's cultured Bengali accent. And I would be back with her at one of the engagement ceremonies that occurred with daunting frequency in our large extended family, though now that Father was gone, we attended fewer of them. It embarrassed me terribly, the way she wiped delicately at her eyes with her white lace handkerchief before pronouncing the words. I was a teenager and easily embarrassed, and if there were people around whose opinion I valued—the glamorous cousins who lived on Hungerford or Park Street and wore European makeup, or school friends with older brothers who knew to whistle the latest Beatles tunes—my embarrassment turned to rage. *How the hell would you know,* I'd long to shout into her face, which was still beautiful in its resigned, aristocratic way, and curiously untouched.

No, I never gave in to that longing.

Where I grew up, you didn't talk to your mother that way, not even when she'd lost what was most important in her life and thus ruined yours. And though my mother and I conversed about many things—my college professors, a new movie, the rising price of Ilish fish—we rarely spoke about what we really thought. We buried our hurts inside our bodies, like shrapnel. We'd been trained well by generations of grandmothers and widow-aunts whose silences weighed down the air of the crumbling ancestral home where we still lived, though now it was too large for the two of us.

There was another thing. I loved my mother, although I would never have admitted it then. Even as I promised myself I wouldn't ever be like her, staking my happiness on a man's whims, I held myself wire-taut to protect her from harm.

In believing I could do this, I was my mother's daughter—sentimental, stubborn, foolish. Exactly how foolish my mother showed me by slipping from my grasp into death.

SHE DID THIS the way she did everything (everything unrelated to my father, that is)—gracefully, with the illusion of ease, like a swimmer entering a warm pool. As though it didn't hurt at all.

FOR OVER A year after my mother's death, I couldn't stand to hear her name. Then one day I found myself thinking of her without the blood slamming around inside my skull. I was thinking of the saying she had liked so much, and how, ironically, her death had proved its corollary: the loss of love, even if it's not a good man's, can kill you. That was what it had done, the cancer which wove its insidious tendrils through her lungs, and which she had managed to keep secret from me almost until the end. The cancer that had begun, old Dr. Biswas told me unwillingly when I confronted him after her death, two years back.

Which was when my father had abandoned her—and me—for a new life in America.

MOTHER USED TO say, *The stars are the eyes of the dead.*

I think of this sometimes when, after tucking Bijoy into his crib, Dilip and I go out onto our night porch. We slump into the railing with the pleased exhaustion familiar to lovers and to parents of young children. Dilip's arm is cool against mine, and smooth as eucalyptus wood. The sprinklers come on, we hear invisible arcs of spray rising and falling, moving in predetermined rhythms across the garden. His skin smells like the watered earth. If she were really looking down on us, my mother would be pleased to see that over the years I've come to accept much of what she tried to teach me. That saying, for example, about a good man's love.

I guess I have to thank Dilip for that.

By the time I met him in graduate school, I had decided I was never going to get married. A good time, yes. Affairs, yes. I already had a few to my credit. But *I* would be the one in control, I warned the men I went out with, the one to say good-bye. When they asked why, I shrugged. Sometimes, the way one presses on a broken bone to check its healing, I told them briefly of my father's departure. About my mother I did not speak. I watched that slight shift in their gaze which signaled pity—or a new and sudden desire, and smiled as a tourist might, just passing through.

But Dilip said, "Monisha, what your father did, why does it have to affect us?"

We were standing under the coppery brightness of a streetlamp outside my apartment building. I looked into his face, its perplexity, and felt that perhaps he was right. That perhaps happiness, which I'd given up on, was an uncharted possibility, a brave geography worth the long effort of exploration.

I DIDN'T ALWAYS disagree with Mother's sayings. Here's one I knew intuitively to be true long before my life proved it so: *Out of bluest sky, lightning strikes.*

So I'm not really surprised when one morning in our calm California kitchen, as I'm feeding Bijoy, Dilip puts his hand over the mouthpiece of the phone and says, "It's your father."

What does surprise me is the hate, welling up from someplace in me I didn't know was there. Since he left us, I had only heard from my father once, a letter, five years back, when I was about to get married. How he found the address of the apartment I shared with two other students

I never did discover. I guess in America there are ways, if you have enough money. He wanted to attend my wedding. I wrote back a polite, definite no. The sophisticated tone of my refusal convinced me that I had overcome the rage of my adolescent years.

Now my hand shakes so hard that I have to put down the spoon.

"Monisha," Dilip says. "He wants to visit his grandson. For his first birthday."

"No," I say, and I pull Bijoy's cereal-sticky hands over my ears so I will not have to hear any more.

But of course I hear. I hear Dilip, courteous as always, say, "I'll have to get back to you, sir." Hear him coming across the kitchen floor toward me.

"No. No. No," I shout.

"It's okay, Mona," Dilip says. "Shhh, it's okay." He puts his hands on mine.

I sit there in my kitchen, streaks of cereal drying on my cheek, holding on to my husband's hands as if he could save me. And I cry as I haven't cried since that day at Nimtola crematorium when I watched mother's body burn.

But I'm not crying for her. I'm crying because all this time I believed I had cured myself of shame—only to have my father show me, with a single phone call, that it wasn't so.

———

IT IS MY favorite time, just after lovemaking, when darkness petals around our bed, holding us in its center. Our moist breaths are mingled; our damp limbs have fallen where they will, unselfconscious, as though we are one body.

Then Dilip says, "He's an old man."

There's a taste in my mouth like rust and illness.

I make myself run my fingertips in little circles over his chest. Perhaps if I act as though I didn't hear, the moment can be salvaged, a little.

But Dilip says, "Mona, listen to me. Bijoy is his only grandchild. He wants to see him before he dies. Surely you can understand that."

I jerk my hand away and pull up the bedsheet to cover me.

"I know you blame him for the hardships you had to go through after he left. And you have the right to—"

You bet I do, I want to shout. The sheet is thick and inescapable, a casing of ice. *You bet I do. The bastard killed my mother.* It's something I've never said aloud, not to myself, and certainly not to Dilip, who knows nothing of my mother except that she is dead.

"But can't you put it behind you?" Dilip is saying.

Easy for you to say, I think as I stare at my husband,

his face so earnest and wholesome that it's clear nothing has ever happened in his life to make him understand what shame is. But perhaps it is only a woman who can realize that word truly.

Suddenly I want to hurt Dilip. I want him to know this gritty tightness in the lungs, like inhaled ash.

"After all, that was a long time ago, in another country—"

The tightness explodes, spraying the air with cinders. It takes me a moment to figure out that it's me, laughing.

"Mona, Mona," Dilip is trying to put his arms around me. "Calm down, please."

" 'And, besides,' " I gasp as I push him from me, " 'the wench is dead.' "

My scientist husband looks at me, bewildered.

"Shakespeare," I say. "*As You Like It.* Put it on your reading list."

Then I snatch up the pillow and go into the guest room.

HERE'S ANOTHER SAYING: *Anger is the great destroyer.* In that last year when she knew she was dying, and I didn't, Mother had cause to say it to me often. I think she got it out of some holy text. They were the only books she read anymore.

She may have been right about anger. I don't deny it. Any more than I deny that I'd become excruciating to live with since Father left. I was like the mansha cactus that grows in the crannies of ruined buildings. Only, my thorns pointed inward, a constant stinging. I lashed out at people every chance I got. It was the only way I knew of consuming pain.

Anger is the great destroyer. Maybe. But I thought of it as my savior.

If Mother had had more anger in her, a voice that beat inside her bones on sleepless nights, *Son of a pig, I refuse to let you ruin my life,* perhaps she would still be alive.

After Mother died, anger was the drug that dulled the throbbing in my head long enough for me to tell solicitous relatives that, no, I wasn't going to move in with any of them, and, no, I didn't really care what people thought of an unmarried girl living alone. It steadied my hand when later I wrote in university applications that I had no relatives in America and was therefore eligible for a student visa. It disconnected me from the need to weep when I sold my mother's jewelry and all her silk saris except one for ticket money.

THE SARI I didn't sell was frayed and ivoried, with a traditional red border. Mother wore it every morning to say her prayers. When I was little I sat by her and played with its crinkly fabric while she rang the brass bell shaped like Hanuman the monkey god. Sometimes I pressed my face into its odors: sandalwood incense and the pungent marigolds Mother offered to the gods in hope of happiness.

WHEN I CHOSE anger, did I have to pay a price?

I'll reply with another question: Don't we all have to pay, no matter what we choose?

OVER DINNER DILIP says, "I have to call him back soon."

I push back my half-eaten dinner and pick up my glass. "Once I met a man. I thought he was smart and sensitive. Caring. That was why I married him—"

"Please, Mona. Don't go all clever and sarcastic on me. Consider carefully. You may regret it one day."

"I thought we'd finished discussing this." My face feels stiff, like it's sprayed with starch. One more word might make it crack.

"How about Bijoy? Doesn't he deserve something, a photo to remember his grandfather by. . . ."

Until I feel the pain in my hand I don't realize how

hard I've set the glass down. The shards make jagged pat-
terns on the table. The spilled water soaks through my
skirt, surprisingly cold. There's a small gash on my palm
from which an inordinate amount of blood wells. Dilip
reaches out in dismay. He's saying something. But I hear my
mother: *Bad luck follows glass breaking.*

My mother had been meticulous in her housekeeping.
All the glasses in our house shone, even the ones we never
used, like the lead crystal set Father brought back from a
long-ago business trip to Europe. Once a month she would
take them out and wash them in soda water. She'd use an
old pink toothbrush to scrub out the grime that accumu-
lates on everything in Calcutta, working lovingly around
the ridges and grooves. When I watched her turning a
glass around in her elegant, capable hands, I knew she
would keep it safe, protected forever from falling. Like she
kept me.

"Don't talk to me about remembering," I say.

DILIP SWEEPS AWAY the glass pieces and bandages my
hand. He gives Bijoy his night bottle. He says, Listen, I'm
really sorry, I won't bring it up again. Says, Come to bed,
Mona, at least try to sleep. Says, Talk to me, please, how
can I understand if you don't talk to me?

This is what I don't tell him:

When she realized Father wasn't coming back, my mother went to the china cabinet. She took out a crystal glass, weighed it thoughtfully in her palm. Behind her I held my breath, fearing and wanting it at once, the crash, the pieces exploding into a violent diamond light. But after some time she called the maid and told her to wrap the set carefully and put it in a box. Tomorrow she would send it to the Loreto orphanage, where the nuns held a yearly auction.

"Make sure you don't use newspaper," said my mother. "The print will leave stains."

I STAND UNOBSERVED in the corridor, watching Dilip and Bijoy play crocodile.

This is how they do it: Dilip lies facedown on the carpet while Bijoy crawl-climbs onto his back. Then Dilip gives a shake and Bijoy rolls off, shrieking with laughter, and an enormous, goofy grin appears on Dilip's face. They've done it about twenty times already and show no signs of tiring.

Watching, I think I understand why my easygoing husband has been so insistent about my father coming to visit. It has less to do with my father than with the idea of fatherhood, what it means to him.

When there's a moment of quiet I say, "He can come the week after Bijoy's birthday. He can stay one night."

Dilip half-rises, a startled movement. Bijoy loses his balance, bumps his head, and begins to cry. I pick him up and kiss him.

"Are you sure?" asks Dilip. "Maybe it's best not to—"

"Dinner's ready," I interrupt. To Bijoy, who's still sobbing, I give another kiss. "Everyone falls," I tell him. "Everyone gets hurt. That's the way it is."

WHY DID I change my mind?

I could say I did it for Dilip, but I suspect there is more to it. Did watching my husband and son at play remind me of a time when my father and I, too, had done the same? When he had carried me on his back around a veranda, shaking his head, making improbable horse noises? Had swung me around in the cool brightness of a garden while greens and yellows blurred into a stream of gold?

No. I have no early memories of my father at all. Whether this is because he was never around, or because I have, with a certain subconscious severity, wiped him from my mind, I am not sure.

But perhaps my first mistake lies in trying to find motive, in thinking of humans as rational beings whose actions spring from logical causes.

For years I tortured myself by trying to uncover the reason beneath my father's leaving. He had grown tired of the trapped sameness of days in a house built by his great-grandfather, I told myself. He had been lured to America by visions of gleaming glass and steel. He had discovered that he no longer loved his wife—that he had never loved her. Or his daughter.

Now I think it might have been more simple than that. (But maybe it is a different word I am reaching for—*random*, or *mysterious*.) Could be, if I had asked him, my father wouldn't have been able to give me an answer, even if he wanted to. Just as I cannot say why I am going against every instinct to let him back into my life.

I HAVE DECIDED I will not go to any trouble to prepare for my father's visit. I want him to know that I don't care about impressing him. So when the doorbell rings that afternoon, my living room is in disarray, the carpet littered with baby books and teething rings, the window-glass sticky with small handprints just where the light hits it most.

Too late I see that I've done it all wrong. I should have covered the table in designer batiks. I should have dressed Bijoy in his embroidered birthday kurta. I should have put on my reddest lipstick and my highest heels, forcing my father to look up, amazed and vexed by the daughter who made a success of her life in spite of him.

But already Dilip's key is rattling in the lock. Breathless,

I reach for Bijoy. *My talisman.* But even as I think the words a terrible objectivity descends on me. For the first time I see my son as a stranger might: a thin, dark-skinned child, quite unremarkable, with a smudge of lunchtime ketchup on his chin.

Distressed, I kiss Bijoy over and over. You're the best boy in the world, I whisper in fierce apology. But a faint bitterness, like seawater, will not leave my mouth.

Perhaps all parents go through this betrayal of vision. But for mine I blame my father.

LATER I WILL try to remember how it felt, the moment when the door swung open, invading the room with the smell of jasmine, facing me with my father.

A note on jasmine: In Bengal, it is considered an erotic flower, a favorite at weddings. Summer evenings, after the day's unbreathable heat, women sit on cool, washed terraces and braid it into their hair. Mother used to do that sometimes, though not after Father left, when there was no longer a reason for her to be beautiful.

Early in her marriage, Mother had had jasmines planted all through our garden. Even that last year, when the rest of the yard was choked by weeds, she'd go downstairs to pick the wilted flowers off the vines.

When she died, I ordered enough jasmine garlands to

cover the entire funeral bed. Shocked relatives whispered their disapproval of such an inappropriate gesture—and so extravagant, too, from a girl who didn't even have a dowry.

WHEN WE WERE looking to buy this house, I told Dilip that the jasmine vines that covered the porch would have to go.

"But, Mona, that's what makes the house so beautiful!"

"They have to go." I knew how I sounded. Petulant. Pigheaded.

But maybe Dilip heard something else. "If it matters that much to you," he said, "they can go."

Once, in a letter I wrote Dilip but never gave him, I said, you have been the anchor of my sanity.

At my mother's pyre, as the only family member present, I'd had to put the torch to her body. Burning, the jasmines gave out a smell like bitter oil.

The day after Dilip and I moved into our new house, I'd gone out to the garden armed with shears. But when I touched the leaves, their glossy, vibrating green, I couldn't do it.

I like to think that my mother is happy about this when she looks down on our porch with her star-steadfast gaze.

BUT HERE IS my father, standing on my doorstep after ten years. It is a moment I've dreaded and longed for, that I've daydreamed over and over.

In the dream my father looks just as he did on that last day, elegant in a pencil-thin mustache, wearing a navy blue suit so new its creases could cut your hands. He is about to step into the taxi that is to drive him to the airport. The reason he has to take a taxi is because Mother has given Hari Charan, our chauffeur, the day off. (Does she believe this will stop my father from leaving?) My mother, who has wept and pleaded since morning, now stands silent on the upstairs veranda. My father faces carefully ahead. Perhaps in his mind he is already gone. He has with him one small suitcase, even though Air India allows him two large ones, as if there's not much that is worth taking from his old life into his new one.

I digress. All this is merely reality, not part of my daydream.

In the dream my father asks if he can come in. Certainly, I say, smiling graciously. Dangerously. He doesn't notice. When he steps forward I slam the door—thwack of wood on flesh, crack of bone—in his face.

BUT THIS FATHER, on this unsuitably beautiful spring day, ambushes me. How old he is, his head shiny with hairlessness, his loose-skinned face where I cannot find any traces of the man I hated. I stare at him as he leans on a cane and peers through thick glasses with the anxiousness of the aged. When he asks if he may come in, the words whirl around inside my head, dizzying me.

Then everything happens at once. Dilip appears, lugging two enormous suitcases. (Why? My father's only supposed to stay a single night.) Bijoy squirms down from my grasp and takes a step—his first. Dilip says, "He walked! He *walked*, did you see that?" My father drops his cane and bends to catch Bijoy just as he loses his balance. "You smart, beautiful boy! How did you know to come to Grandpa?" A smile moves across his face, full and unhurried, like molasses, strengthening my sense that this isn't really my father. I find that I, too, am smiling at this old man's pleasure in my son.

Then he straightens and says, almost in surprise, "You're beautiful too, and so much like—"

He bites his lip, but it's too late. The unspoken words rise in a jagged line between us like the broken glass embedded into our compound walls back home to keep out thieves.

I HAVE NOT been totally honest in stating that I'd done nothing to prepare for my father. I'd put a vase of jasmine on the bedside table in the guest room. And I'd ironed my mother's sari to wear to dinner.

IT'S AFTER DINNER and I'm at the kitchen sink, ostensibly doing dishes. I rattle spoons to create an impression of diligence, but in truth I'm watching my father.

At dinner he looked at the sari as though he'd never seen it in his life and complimented me on the chicken curry. He said the guest room was very pretty. Is my father tougher than I've imagined? Or—this possibility fills me with dismay—has he forgotten all I remember?

In the family room my father opens his cases and lifts out toys. Bright Snurf balls, Playskool blocks, Mattel trucks in every size, some operated by remote controls that look unnervingly like guns. He has brought batteries too, my father who believes in leaving nothing to chance, and now he triumphantly aims the remote at a red-and-white ambulance which comes to life with a screech and a flashing of lights.

I tighten my hands into fists to stop myself from covering my ears. The wail of the ambulance is a black hole through which I'm tumbling into the afternoon when I found my mother doubled over with pain in the easy chair on the veranda. I'd called for an ambulance at once. But there was a strike in Calcutta that day. Angry protesters marched along the street in front of our house, shouting, carrying placards demanding the resignation of some high-up official whose name I've forgotten. The ambulance was caught in the melee—I could see it from the veranda—its lights pulsing a rapid, futile red as its driver tried to navigate his way to our gate.

Bijoy loves his ambulance, though. He picks it up and hugs it, squealing with delight at the spinning wheels. Everyone smiles, even me. Then I notice the clothes. My father has brought a whole wardrobe, little playsuits and onesies and sailor shirts, but also big-boy clothes, neat, buttoned-down shirts a kid could wear on his first day at kindergarten, a baseball outfit complete with catcher's mitt, a white jacket for a summer piano recital.

It comes to me that he is afraid this visit—his first—is also his last. The clothes are his hopes for his grandson's life. He doesn't expect me to allow him to return, to share with Bijoy any of the things they promise.

For a moment I see myself as he must: the daughter who carries a mountain of grudges on her shoulder, vengeful as any evil fairy in a childhood tale, and as filled with power. Can I say he is entirely wrong?

The thought is a jolt, so sharp and physical that it makes me drop the bowl I have been soaping. Glass shatters loudly all over the sink.

"Are you okay, Mona?" Dilip asks. "Did you cut your-self again?"

I barely hear him. It's my father's gaze I'm aware of, the eyes which have widened slightly at that *again*. Under their scrutiny I dwindle, no evil fairy but a clumsy teenager once more, left behind because I'm not worth taking along. I mumble something about being just fine, about getting the rubber gloves for cleanup, and escape down the corridor.

ON THAT LAST day in Calcutta I stood on the veranda next to my mother, ready to tell my father something suit-ably acerbic that I'd been rehearsing all day. I would call this out when he turned to wave us good-bye, I'd decided, and it would humiliate him into staying. But he hadn't turned.

As he walked toward the taxi with that ridiculously small suitcase, my father's whole body leaned forward in ter-rible eagerness, as though he were a patient discharged from a hospital he never thought he'd live to leave.

When the taxi took off with a belch of black fumes, my mother moaned softly. It was an eerie, nonhuman sound. I felt it taking shape in my own throat, the way one wolf might as it watches another one howl.

It was my duty as a daughter to comfort my mother. A part of me longed to do it. But what could I say to a woman brought up on sayings like *The husband is God*? Whose elders had blessed her since childhood by saying, *May you never become a widow.* Who believed—as I, too, did on some unacknowledged level—that tragic though widowhood was, abandonment was worse.

I said to my mother, in my coldest voice, "For heaven's sake, pull yourself together." I turned on my heel and walked away.

I'M NOT SURE how long I spend in the bathroom, staring at the cleaning supplies. By the time I come out, the family room's surprisingly quiet. I peer around the corner, taking care not to be seen.

Bijoy's fallen asleep in Dilip's lap, limbs flung out in the uncaring absoluteness of sleeping children. The two men are watching him. From time to time they speak in whispers.

My father puts out his hand and rubs Bijoy's foot. I know how it feels, the soft, unblemished sole, the budlike toes, the smooth fit of that ankle in the curve of a palm. What I haven't counted on is how *I* feel, this swift welling of a joy I don't fully understand.

My father is speaking slowly, slurredly, each word a stone placed on his tongue. "People do things, you know. They want something so badly, every minute feels like they're being held down underwater. Then years later they look back and can't believe they could ever have felt anything so strongly. . . ."

I'm suddenly furious. What he did, no amount of talk can make it right. He'd taken my mother's life, precious and fragile as this silk I am wearing, and ripped it apart. And now he wanted the easy solace of confession.

I clatter down the passage, purposely loud. Maybe I'm afraid, too, not ready to hear something that might confuse my loyalties. So I busy myself with picking Bijoy up.

"I'll put him in his crib and then go to bed myself," I say. "I'm exhausted. I'll clean up tomorrow. Good night." I say all this very quickly, so that my father will not have a chance to complete what he started to say.

But as I carry Bijoy away, breathing in his milk-and-talcum smell, clean and uncomplicated, I hear him behind me.

"Except regret," says my father.

SINCE BIJOY'S BIRTH I've learned to wake at his first cry, to be at his crib before he can replenish his lungs. Sometimes I smile at the irony of it, I whom my mother used to tease about my love of sleep.

Tonight when Bijoy cries, Dilip says, "I'll get up. It's been a hard day for you."

"No, thanks," I say shortly. "You've done enough already." I'm annoyed at how amiable my husband has been toward my father, and I want him to know it. Besides, I have no wish to give up these treasured night moments with my son.

Now I bend over Bijoy's crib, thinking how easily my body assumes this familiar stoop, how easily an old tune out of my childhood, *Chhele ghumolo, para jurolo, Baby sleeps, the neighborhood is peaceful at last*, hums itself from my throat. I stroke my son out of his nightmare and into sleep again, until his muscles soften under my hand.

I want one of my mother's sayings, something that will encapsulate this moment of parenthood in its exact glow, but what comes to me is quite different.

I HAVE PRESENTED myself inaccurately as the lone connoisseur of Shakespeare in my family.

Long ago, before a husband's desires and a child's needs usurped her life, my mother had gone to college. Like me, she had studied English, though she had quit uncomplainingly, good daughter that she was, when it was time for her to marry.

I had forgotten this. Or perhaps, self-absorbed as children alone can be, I had never really believed that my mother had an existence of her own before I was born.

This is how I was reminded:

When our relatives knew that Father had left, they descended upon us in hordes, armed with sympathy and suggestions which made me smart for days. The worst was Ila Mashi, mother's cousin. "How could you let him go?" she'd say. "*Now* what's going to happen to you two? He hasn't been sending money either, has he?" Or "Monisha should write him a letter begging him to come back, or at least to arrange for your green cards."

I refused to give her the satisfaction of a response. But after she left, I'd berate my mother bitterly. Did she have no self-respect? No backbone? If I were her, I wouldn't let Mashi into my house again.

"What to do," Mother said. "Sometimes you have to forgive people."

"Forgive! *Forgive!* Next you'll be telling me you've forgiven my father for what he did."

"I haven't," said my mother. "But I keep trying. I have to, more for you and me than for him."

I wasn't sure what she meant by that last part, but I didn't like it. "Keep me out of it," I said. "And let me tell you something. That man doesn't deserve forgiveness."

She'd stood up straight then and looked at me, earnest in her desire—the desire of all mothers, I know that now—to give her child something vital to navigate her life by.

"Give every man what he deserves," said my mother, pulling the half-remembered words haltingly out of her youth, that time when everything had seemed graspable, "and who shall 'scape whipping."

BIJOY SLEEPS CURLED on his side, knees drawn up, hands tucked under his chin. Watching him, I marvel again at the uniqueness of it. Neither Dilip nor I sleep this way. Once Dilip told me that probably lots of babies did that, we were just too inexperienced to know. I nodded, but I wasn't convinced. I knew my son was special.

I could stand here all night watching him, this child already with secrets to his life, dreaming things I'll never know. But I think of having to face my father at breakfast. I'm going to need all the rest I can get. I cover Bijoy with his quilt and close the door.

That's when I notice the light coming from the guest room.

No, I say to myself. No, Monisha. Let things be. But already I am walking down the corridor.

WHAT DO I want as I walk to the room where my father lies sleepless?

The answer: I wish I knew.

I have a vague notion of confrontation, accusation, of perhaps tears. (His, not mine.) My head is congested with images I need him to see: my mother's face, gaunt with sickness; the broker bringing strings of prospective buyers to the house; the day I sent the servants away because there was no more money; my hand setting the pyre alight, those jasmines burning.

All the things he walked away from, leaving them for me.

ONCE AGAIN I'VE misjudged. My father is not tossing, guilt-ridden, on his bed of thorns. He's asleep. He just hasn't switched off the lamp.

I venture closer to see why. He'd been reading when sleep struck him down, so suddenly that he didn't have a chance to remove his glasses or cover himself. The red cloth-bound book splayed by the pillow looks just like the holy texts mother used to read before she died.

There's an irony in this somewhere, but as I try to figure it out, my eyes fall on my father's face. How different it seems in repose, the tension melted out of it. I see that he's been afraid of this trip as much as I have. Maybe that's why he hasn't removed the vase of jasmine from the bedside table but merely pushed it all the way to the edge.

The night has grown colder, and my father sleeps curled

on his side with his knees drawn up. Denuded of fear, his face could be an adolescent's, soft-chinned and self-willed.

And for a moment I'm looking into the core of my father's existence, who he was. Is. The boy-prince I read of in the old tales, his face always turned toward adventure. The prince who never grew up, who, trapped by the mundane demands of a household, believed he could free himself with a single, graceful slash of his sword.

Not so different from me, slashing through life with anger as my weapon of choice, after all.

I lift the glasses from his face, shake out a blanket over him. I'm careful not to touch him. But his eyes flutter open. I hold my breath until I realize that he's still mostly asleep. Even if he saw, it would only be a blur of white and red, my mother's sari which I am wearing.

I lift the jasmines from the vase and hurry toward the door intent on escape.

Then I hear my father call out a sleep-softened word. Is it my mother's name? Someone else's? I wait for the prickly heat to rise up under my skin, but there's just a slight tingling. When did the answer cease to matter as much?

It's only a little thing. I cannot call it forgiveness.

My mother would have disagreed. She'd have said, *Ocean is nothing but water drop upon water drop.* And if I said, I don't know if I'll ever have more than this one drop to give, she'd have smiled.

My father sighs and turns, tucking his hands neatly, familiarly, under his chin.

I switch off the lamp and close the door. In my grasp the jasmine stems are tough and knuckled, like fingers. I think I will start collecting sayings of my own. *Invisible flowers spread greater fragrance. Home is where you move fluently through the dark.* In our bedroom Dilip is lying awake. When I reach him, I'll begin to tell him about my mother. How she died. What she lived by.

It's a story that has waited a long time.

WHAT THE BODY KNOWS

WHEN HER WATER breaks, Aparna is standing on a chair in the baby room, hanging up the ceramic flying-fish mobile Umesh and she had purchased the day before. As the wetness gushes out of her, warm and unpleasantly sticky, she notes for one wondering moment the instinctive reactions of her body—the panic drying her mouth, the legs clamping together as though by doing so they could prevent loss. Then terror takes over, sour and atavistic—just what she had been determined not to succumb to, all through the carefully planned months of doctors visits and iron pills and baby-care books and Lamaze classes. It floods her brain and she cannot think.

She drops the mobile and hears it hit the tile floor with a splintery crash. Somewhere in the back of her mind there is regret, but her body has suddenly grown clumsy, and all her energies must go into getting down from the chair. She negotiates the newly dangerous floor to the kitchen where Umesh is fixing an omelette just the way she likes it, with lots of onions and sliced green chilies. She can smell their crisp, buttery odor. She opens her mouth to say he's the best husband—No, it's something else she must tell him, only she can't recall what.

But already he's abandoned the omelette and rushed across the room.

"Aparna, sweetheart, are you okay? You look awfully pale." And then, as she holds her stomach, the words still lost, "No, it can't be! It's only July—three weeks too early. Are you sure? Does it hurt?"

His face is so scrunched up with anxiety, his eyes so eloquent with guilt, she has to laugh. His fear lessens hers. She puts out her hand to him and the flood in her brain recedes, leaving only a few muddy patches behind. "I'm fine," she says. "My water broke."

She likes the way he fusses over her, making her lie down on the sofa, arranging pillows under her feet. Her long hair falls over the edge of the sofa, glossy and dramatic, hair that might belong to the heroine of a tragedy. Only this isn't a tragedy, it's the happiest event in their lives. Maybe it's a comedy—the way, in his hurry, he misdials the hospital number, getting a Texaco instead. He's sweating by the time he gets the labor ward, shouting into the phone. She smiles. In her mind she's already making up the story she will tell her son. *Do you know what your father did, the day you were born?* She thinks of the hospital bag, has she packed everything the Lamaze instructor listed? Yes, even the sourballs she is supposed to suck on during labor—she picked them up on her last trip to the grocery, just in case. She feels pleased about that.

All through the ride to the hospital the sky is a scrubbed-clean, holiday blue, echoing the Niles lilies that fill the neighboring gardens. She allows her mind the luxury of wandering. Panic comes at her in waves, but she makes her body loose, the way a sea swimmer might, and feels it pass beneath her. How is it she's never noticed all these roses, red and white and a golden yellow the same shade as the baby outfit that lies folded in tissue at the bottom of her hospital bag? She chose green sourballs, lime flavor. They make her mouth pucker in pleasant anticipation. The air is soft against her face, like a baby's cheek.

Later she would wonder, was it better that way, not knowing when death looked over your shoulder? Was it better to confound its breath with the scent of roses? To take that perfect moment and squander it because you were sure you had a thousand more?

THEY'RE TALKING ABOUT stocks, she can hear them quite clearly, although they've draped a curtain of sorts between her and them. Her gynecologist prefers the blue chip kind. IBM, he says as he starts cutting. The anesthesiologist, a young man with a jolly mustache who shook her hand before inserting the needle into her spine, disagrees. The thing is to invest in a good start-up before it goes public. "There's a bunch of them right here in the Valley, right under our noses," he says, and rattles off names.

"I hope you're taking notes," Aparna whispers with mock-seriousness to Umesh. "It'll put the kid through college." Then she shudders as the doctor slices into a particularly stubborn piece of tissue.

Umesh's hands on her arm are slick with sweat. She can see the thin red traceries of veins in his eyes. He has been biting his lips ever since they said they'd have to operate, the baby's heartbeats didn't sound so good. She feels an illogical need to comfort him.

"Are you hurting?" he leans forward to ask. "Shall I ask them to do something about it?"

She shakes her head. Through all the pulling and cutting, her flesh being rent apart and then stitched together like old leather, there's an amazing absence of pain. But the body knows, she thinks. You can't fool the body. It knows what's being done to it. At the right time, it will take revenge.

Now they're laying the baby on her chest, the compact solidness of him, the face red and worried, like his father's. But beautiful, not discolored and cone-shaped from being pushed out of the birth-tunnel as in the Lamaze videos, so that she feels a bit better about having the C-section. She thinks of the name she chose for him. Aashish. Blessing. Even though the spinal is wearing off and pain begins to flex its muscles, she holds on to that word.

Unlike the squalling infants in the birth videos she's watched, her baby gazes at her with self-possession. She's been told that newborns can't focus, but she knows better. Her baby sees her, and likes what he sees. If only they would leave the two of them alone to get to know each other. But a uniformed somebody swoops him up out of her arms with foolish, clucking sounds. Umesh is saying something equally foolish about bringing him back when she's rested. Can't they see she's quite rested and wants him *now*? She hates hospitals, she thinks with a sudden starburst of energy, always has. She can't wait to get out of this one and never come back.

THE NIGHT SHE returns home, Aparna wakes in the dark, early hours with a sentence running through her head. *I think of pain as the most faithful of my friends.* It takes her a while to place it. It's from a diary, a woman writer she read in a long-ago class in early American literature. She didn't trust that woman, forgot her name as soon as she could.

But now Aparna must admit she knows what the writer had meant. Pain is with Aparna constantly, lurking beneath the lavender-scented sheets of the king-size bed she and Aashish have taken over. Different from the ache she felt in the hospital, it gnaws at her like a giant rat.

"How lovely!" the visitors say. "Look at the roses in her cheeks! It's wonderful to see someone so happy!"

She snaps at Umesh when he feels her hot, dry forehead and asks if he can get her something. When he calls, the doctor says pain is normal—just as normal as new fathers worrying too much.

She will conquer pain by ignoring it, Aparna resolves. For three shimmery days of learning to breast-feed Aashish, she focuses on the shape of him in the crook of her arm, the blunt tug of his gums on her swollen nipples. But one morning when she climbs out of bed to try to use the toilet, which is becoming increasingly difficult, she falls and cannot get up.

SHE WILL ALWAYS remember the moment when she swims up out of delirium, which spreads around her like a bottomless lake, shining like mercury. It's hard to focus her eyes, but driven by an unnamed fear she forces herself to do so. It's evening. She's in the hospital. In the very same room where she was before. Has all this in-between time been a dream, then? But the space next to her bed where the bassinet stood, against the cheerful peach wall, is empty. *Where's my baby,* she screams, *what did you do with my baby?* The words come out as gurgles through the tubes in her nose and mouth. The nurse bends over her, so cow-faced in her ignorance that Aparna must shake some sense into her— until they tie down her hands and give her a shot.

Then Umesh is there, explaining that she was too ill to take care of Aashish, so he's at a friend's house while the doctors try to figure out what's wrong with her. He understands her meaningless grunts and sobs. "Please don't worry, we'll all be fine," he says, stroking the insides of her elbows, the thin ache of needles plunged in and taped over, until she stops trembling and her eyes don't dart around as much. "Calm down, sweetheart, I'll hold you till you sleep." He tells her how well Aashish is doing, gaining weight every day, how he turns his head at sounds, how hard he can kick. She even smiles a little as she falls asleep in the middle of a question she wants to ask, *When can I go home?* In sleep she thinks she hears his murmured answer. *Soon, darling.* His voice is cool and breathable, like night mist. But when she wakes, she's in the middle of the mercury lake. She flails her way up, there's that gaping space by her bed again, and she screams.

APARNA HAS NEVER been an angry person. It amazes her, therefore, when in the brief moments of clarity between panic and the dull cottony stupor of medication, she feels fury swelling her organs, as tangible as all the fluids her body has forgotten how to get rid of. She's been here for two weeks now, with test after inconclusive test being run on her. Everything in this hospital enrages her. The gluey odor of the walls. The chalky liquid she has to choke down so machines can take a clearer picture of her insides. The pretty, polished faces of the young nurses who chose the ob-stetrics ward so they would have happy patients. Her gy-necologist's smile as he says they'll soon have her good as new. Aparna wants to punch his teeth in. She wants a lawyer who'll sue him for every stock he owns. She wants a hit man who'll wipe that smile off the face of the earth.

When they tell her she has to have a second surgery, she cries in great, gulping sobs, letting the snot and tears mingle on her face. She's too tired to wipe them away, and, besides, what's the point? She's ugly, she knows it, with her hair matted and smelly around her face. Ugly as sin, having to wear that hospital gown which exposes her backside. Having them hold her head when, periodically, she throws up bowlfuls of greenish scum. Having them clean her up afterward. That's the worst, somehow, the dispassionate way in which a stranger's hand moves over her body, doing its job. She's defeated by pain, she finally admits it. That evening when Umesh comes to visit, she turns her head away and won't look at the Polaroid photos he's taken of Aashish being given his bath.

ALTHOUGH THE SURGERY has been successful, and the intestinal adhesions that had caused all the problems have been removed, Aparna's recovery is not going well. They're worried about it. She knows this from the flurries of whispers when the doctors come to see her each day. There's a whole team of them, her gynecologist, the surgeon who performed the second surgery, an immunologist, and even a social worker, a gnatlike woman who has informed Aparna that she is one of her cases now. They poke and prod, examine her stitches and her charts, ask questions which she doesn't answer. Until they walk away, she keeps her eyes

tightly closed against them. This way, if she ever gets better and meets them, say, in a shopping mall, she won't know
who they are. She'll walk right past them with the polite,
powerful unconcern only a stranger is capable of.

Once she hears the night nurse talking to Umesh about
her. This nurse is an older woman, not foolishly chirpy like
the others. In her pre-hospital days, when she had energy for
such things, Aparna would have equipped her with a complete, imagined life: She had lost her family, husband and all
four children, in the Los Angeles earthquake, and moved to
the Bay Area, where she now worked nights because she
couldn't stand to be home alone. Or perhaps she'd been in
Vietnam and seen things the young nurses couldn't even
imagine. That's why she watched them with that slightly
sardonic expression as they cooed over their patients, bringing cranberry juice and tucking down comforters. But the
present, eroded Aparna only knows that the night nurse is
comfortable with death. She knows it from the way the nurse
sometimes comes in after lights-out and massages Aparna's
feet, leaning there in a dark that smells thick and sticky, like
hospital lotion, without speaking a single word.

But now, outside the door, the nurse is speaking to
Umesh. "She's lost the will to live," she says in her dour,
gravelly way.

"But why?" asks Umesh. His voice is high and bewildered, like a child's. "How can she, when she has so much to live for?"

"It happens."

"I won't let it," Umesh says angrily. "I won't. There must be something I can do."

Aparna listens with faint curiosity, the way one might to a TV soap playing in the next room. Does the wise nurse have a solution which will revitalize the dispirited young mother and unite her once more with her caring husband and helpless infant?

"You must—" says the nurse. But what he must do is drowned in the excited exclamations of a family who arrive just then in the room next to Aparna's to view their newest member.

SHE SHOULD HAVE known what they were planning. But the medication has turned her mind soft, like butter left out overnight, so that the things she wants to hold on to—questions and suspicions—sink into it and disappear. Still, she shouldn't have been so utterly shocked when her friend walked in carrying Aashish.

A few times before this, Umesh had tried to get her to see Aashish. But each time he suggested it, she wept so vehemently that her temperature went up and the nurse had to give her a shot. Afterward, he would stroke the ragged ends of her hair with distressed hands and say, "Please, please, Aparna. Don't act this way. Be reasonable." She did not want to be reasonable. He had no right to ask her to be. An enormous, thwarted emotion ballooned inside her chest whenever she thought of her lost baby—*lost*, yes, that was the right word. She felt it pushing into her lungs, displacing air, long after Umesh gave up and left.

She watches them now, her friend who looks anxious as she sets the car seat down and picks up Aashish. Aashish in a little red two-piece outfit that Aparna didn't buy for him. Aashish looking so grown and cheerful that Aparna can hardly believe he's hers. But that's it, he *isn't* her baby. Something terrible happened to her own baby because she was in the hospital and couldn't take care of him, and they're afraid to tell her. So they've brought in this . . . this little impostor. *Where's my baby?* she wants to ask. *What did you do with my baby?* Instead she says, in a gray, toneless voice, "Take him away."

"At least hold him once," her friend says, and she bends over Aparna to move the tubes out of the way so she can lay the baby beside her. Her eyelashes are spiky with tears. Aparna can smell, in her friend's hair, the woodsy fragrance of Clairol Herbal Essence. It's the same shampoo Aparna used when she was pregnant. Suddenly she longs for the slow, steady green of it pooling in her palm, the relaxing steam of the shower, her fingers—her own fingers—on her scalp, knowing just where to rub deep and where to lighten up.

But here against her side is this baby, kicking his legs, batting at her with his small, fat arms. When she offers him a finger, he grabs it and gives an unexpected, gurgly laugh. Her friend has stepped outside, leaving a bottle of baby formula on the nightstand. "Baby," she whispers—she isn't ready, yet, to speak the name that will claim him as hers—and he laughs again. The sound tugs at the corners of her stiff, unaccustomed mouth until she's laughing, too. His gums are the color of the pink oleanders she planted in her backyard.

Then he's hungry, suddenly and absolutely, the way babies are. He's starting to fuss, in a minute he'll begin crying, she can tell from the way he's squinching up his face. She reaches, hurriedly, for the bottle, then stops, struck by an idea so compelling she can hardly breathe. She glances guiltily at the doorway, but it's empty, so she pulls at her hospital gown until she uncovers a breast and holds it to Aashish's mouth.

Why does Aparna do this? She's aware that she has no milk, although exactly how that occurred is obscured by the cottony fog which hangs over the first few days of her readmission to the hospital. Perhaps this is a test, offering her breast to the baby: *If he's my true, true son, he'll take it.* Perhaps it's the hope of a miracle. She remembers, vaguely, old Indian tales where milk spurts from a mother's breasts when she is reunited with her long-lost children. But mostly it's her body crying out to feel, once more, the hard, focused clamp of those gums.

Aashish will have none of it. He howls, face splotched with red, his body gone rigid. He refuses to be consoled by pats or clucking sounds, so Aparna must reach for the bottle with shaking fingers, afraid that someone will rush in and demand to know just what she's done to the poor child and take him away. In her haste she knocks over the bottle, which rolls under the bed, beyond the reach of her tube-restricted arms. And she must lie there next to her son's crying, a sound that jabs at her like a burning needle, until her friend does, indeed, rush in and take him from her.

LATER, WHEN ALL this is over and Aparna has settled back into the familiar rhythms of her life—but, no, her life, bisected by almost-death into Before and After, will never be familiar again. She will find it subtly altered, like a known melody into which a new instrument has been inserted. Anyhow, when she has settled back, people will ask her, *But what finally made you better?* She will give them different answers. "It was the new antibiotic," she might say, "the Cipro." Or, with a shrug, "I was lucky." Only once will she say, to a friend—not the one who had taken care of her baby; somehow they drifted apart after Aparna got better—she will say, looking out the window and blushing a little, "Love saved me."

"Of course," the friend will reply, nodding her sympathy. "I understand!" But Aparna herself will not be sure if she has been referring to her husband and son, as the friend has surmised, or to something quite different.

A FEW DAYS after the disastrous baby episode, Aparna opens her eyes to find a man in her room. He startles her in his clean-shaven, blond boyishness, this stranger in a T-shirt and jeans. "I'm Dr. Byron Michaels," he says, extending a hand which she ignores. It takes her several minutes to recognize him as the man who performed her second surgery. In his street clothes, he looks so different from the times when he visited her with the rest of the squad that she doesn't close her eyes and turn away, as she originally intended. And though she doesn't return his smile, when he pulls up a chair and settles himself next to her, she watches him with a certain interest.

"I want to tell you," he says, "about your surgery. I think you need to know."

Before she can say, *No, thank you very much,* he has started.

"The other surgeons," he says, talking in the clipped tones of a man who's grown used to being always busy, "didn't want to operate on you. They thought you'd die on the table. But I took it as a challenge. Maybe it was foolish. When I opened you up and saw everything stuck together, I thought, I can't do it. The guy working with me wanted me to stitch you up again. But I was damned if I was going to leave you there to die."

Dr. Michaels's voice slows down. He's looking at her, but Aparna feels he's seeing something else. As he speaks, his hands make small, plucking movements in the air. "I started cleaning the organs, wiping the gunk off them, cutting away the cocoon that covered your intestines. It took hours. I was sweating like crazy. The nurse had to keep wiping my face. Afterward, she had to help me off with my gloves. My legs were shaking so much I had to sit down. But I'd done it."

Through the window, sunlight catches the golden hairs of the surgeon's forearm. His biceps are smooth and convex, like a high school athlete's. Aparna wonders if she is one of his first serious cases.

"And now," he says bitterly, "you're just throwing it all away."

The sunlight is on his cheek now, glowing and insistent. It strikes her that in all her life she's never touched a man's face except for her husband's. She would like to know, before she dies, how this pink, American skin feels. She puts out her hand—she has so little to lose that she isn't embarrassed—and touches his face. It's unexpectedly hot. She thinks she senses a pricking in her fingertips, the slight, tingly pain of circulation returning to a limb. A blush springs up under his skin, but perhaps Byron—through the rest of her hospital stay, that's how she'll think of him, a Romantic poet resurrected in surgical greens—understands, for he sits very still and allows her finger to circle the hollow between his jaw and cheekbone.

SOMETHING HAS CHANGED. Where before Aparna refused to step out of bed, she now goes for walks, shuffling in badly fitting foam hospital slippers alongside a nurse who pushes her IV machine. Where she barely endured with indifference the quick swipe of a washcloth, now she wants to be helped to the bathroom so she can wash her face properly. She asks a delighted Umesh to bring her makeup bag, and each morning with unsteady fingers she applies lipstick and eyeliner and rubs jasmine oil behind her earlobes. When Umesh holds her hands in his and tells her how beautiful she looks, how thankful he is that she's taken such a turn for the better, she smiles distractedly. One night when he kisses her before leaving, murmuring how lonely it is in bed, she finds herself imagining that it is Byron who says this. And thus she is forced to admit to herself the motivation for her improvement.

Byron's visits to her are brief and irregular, sandwiched between surgeries and other, sicker patients. She waits for him with an eagerness that she recognizes as excessive. She does not touch him again, but against her will she finds herself fantasizing about it—and worse. This is humiliating, particularly since he seems to feel nothing but professional interest toward her as he examines her stitches and compliments her on her recovery process.

Aparna tells herself she's behaving stupidly. She's degenerating into a stereotype, the female patient infatuated with her doctor. Surely she's more intelligent than that? She thinks she catches an amused look, once or twice, in a nurse's eye. Stop it! she commands herself. Yet there she is next morning, sitting up in bed lipsticked and ready, trying to comb the knots out of her hair, which she has made the nurse shampoo for her. When the curtain moves, she looks up with her sultriest smile. But it is only Umesh, who wanted to surprise her on his way to work with a bouquet of irises from their garden, and who is baffled by the sulky monosyllables with which she answers him.

IT'S BYRON'S IDEA to bring the baby back. Aparna is reluctant and scared. She blurts out that the previous visit was a disaster, though she cannot bear to share its painful details even with him.

"Try it one more time," he says. He puts a hand on her shoulder. "Try it for me."

This time it's a lot better, once she gets over how big Aashish has grown. He looks nothing like the tiny, swaddled baby she's held on to so tightly inside her head. He doesn't recognize her at all. But that's almost a relief, because now she doesn't have to behave like a mother—she's not sure she'd know how to, after all this time. It's okay for her to be, instead, her awkward, prickly self.

But Aashish has a way of deprickling her. Maybe it's his willingness to be amused by the finger games she invents. He likes it when she brings her face close to his and makes strange noises. When she runs out of noises to make, he watches her unblinkingly—"as though my face were the most interesting thing in the universe," she says in laughing amazement to Umesh.

That intent, considering gaze, that looking out at the world with a pure and complete attention. She is delighted and humbled by it. She, too, wants to learn it. And if (as she fears) she's too old for that, then she wants to be close to her son and learn it through him. So she practices over and over with the breath-blower the nurses have given her, the little balls inside plastic tubes which are supposed to strengthen her lungs. She forces herself to walk a little farther down the corridor each day. She even tries the visualization exercises in the book one of her friends brought, shutting her eyes and willing herself to feel her body glowing with disks of light. She still makes up her face every morning for Byron, still enjoys seeing him. But sometimes as they talk, she finds her mind straying. Those footsteps outside, could that be Umesh, bringing Aashish a little earlier today?

MIRACULOUSLY, THE DAY of her discharge arrives. The nurses make a special occasion of it, chipping in to buy her a baby outfit and a pair of hand puppets. They blow on noisemakers and clap as they wheel her down the corridor for the last time. From the back of the car, she waves at them with one hand as she holds tight to Aashish's car seat with the other. When the car turns the corner, she realizes that she is crying.

Byron came in that morning for a final checkup and pronounced her cured. This isn't exactly true. She still finds it tiring to walk the length of the corridor and back. She has to lower herself into a chair with aggravating slowness.

Though she longs for a nice chili curry, she has been placed on a strict diet: interminable wastelands of applesauce and white bread loom ahead of her. Still, her heart leaped like a fish that had been tossed back into the lake.

Byron held out his hand. She touched it lightly. It was the first time she was touching him since the afternoon he told her how he'd saved her life. She wanted to say something to him about that, about love. But he was telling her he hoped to see her in his office in a week's time, telling her to call his secretary, telling her to watch that diet. He filled up the space between them with mundaneness. When he stopped, she didn't have anything left to say.

QUICK AND SLIM in a black T-shirt and shorts, Aparna moves through the children's section of Macy's, picking up items for Aashish's first birthday. In her cart, in addition to goody-bag gifts for the children she has invited, is a large purple Barney, Aashish's favorite TV character, and a red silk kite in the shape of a fish. She has worked hard to gain back her pre-pregnancy body and has, her friends claim enviously, even more energy than before. There's a new impatience about her, too. At times it makes them uneasy. *Get to the point,* it seems to say. *You don't have as much time as you think.*

Aparna has managed to forget most of what she wanted to forget about her illness. There are a few things. She'll drive a mile out of her way so she doesn't have to pass the squat gray building where she spent a month of her life. She can't stand certain colors—cheery yellow, innocuous peach, cute pink. A particular hour of evening, when shadows the color of bruises cluster under windowsills, makes her stomach clench with anxiety. But she chalks these up as minor costs.

She flings a wave of dark hair over her shoulder and makes for the cash register, a beautiful woman with such confident eyes that people would never guess what she's been through. At that moment she sees Dr. Michaels. He, too, is heading toward the cashier with something bunched up in his hand—a pullover, she thinks, but she is lightheaded with an anguish she thought she had done with, and thus not sure.

She never did go back to see him. She told Umesh it was too painful, all those negative associations. Did he suspect other reasons? If so, he didn't bring them up. There was a wary gentleness to how he handled her requests in those first days, as though she were a glass window. Any refusal would be a rock thrown into it. Thankfully, she thinks with a smile, recalling their energetic arguments about the birthday party, that didn't last too long.

Aparna's first impulse is to duck behind the enormous display of floral bedsheets across the way. But that would be cowardly. Besides, Dr. Michaels has spotted her already and walks up to her with his head slightly cocked, as though he isn't quite sure that she's who she is. She's afraid he'll be accusing or, worse still, sentimental, but he only puts out the hand she knows so intimately—the way we know objects out of our childhood, or our dreams—and touches her on the elbow.

"I'm so glad to see you," he says. "How have you been? And your baby? A boy, wasn't it?"

Aparna struggles to find an intelligent answer. But that touch—it disturbs her, bringing back that long-ago afternoon, her hand on his sun-tinted cheek. The embarrassment she had not felt then floods her face. Then she notices how he's looking at her. Her strong, slender legs, the sheen in her newly washed hair—he gazes at them with the marveling eyes of someone who lives each day with bodies broken by disease.

She feels a rush inside her, but it is different from the clutching, shameful emotion she felt toward him in the hospital. It dizzies her. When she looks up, everything—his face, the bedsheet display, the ceiling of Macy's—is tinged with a tender gold. She wants to tell him that he will always be unique in her life, the man who opened her up and touched the innermost crevices of her body. Who traveled with her, Orpheus-like, the dusky alleyway between life and death.

"I'd love to hear all your news," Dr. Michaels is saying. "Do you have time for coffee?" He's holding her hand in a proprietorial fashion. As though she were still in the hospital, and he still in charge, thinks Aparna with slight annoyance. The look in his eyes has changed, and is easier to read. Once she had sat up in her sickbed, rubbing lipstick into cracked lips, darkening sunken eyes with shaky fingers, longing for such a look from him. Now it fills her with sadness because it reveals him to be no different from other men.

Aparna has time. The party isn't until next week, and being a compulsive planner she has already organized the major details. Aashish, who is at the house of a friend with whom she exchanges child care twice a week, doesn't need to be picked up until afternoon. But she whispers an apology and frees her hand from Dr. Michaels's.

"Maybe at another time, then?" he says. "That might be better—some afternoon when we aren't rushed. For lunch, or maybe drinks? We could go up to San Francisco . . ." He takes out a card, writes a number on the back. "My cell phone," he says. "Call me . . . ?"

She takes the card and inclines her head slightly. It is a gesture not of assent—as he takes it to be, she can tell by his pleased, boyish grin—but of acceptance. The acceptance of frailty—hers and his, their different, inevitable frailties. She will never tell him—or anyone—about how, just a moment ago, everything was touched with gold. Some things can't be spoken. The body alone knows them. It holds them patiently, in its silent, intelligent cells, until you are ready to see.

When, with a jaunty wave, Dr. Michaels turns the corner, she drops his card—but gently—into a garbage can. At the cash register, laying her purchases on the counter, she closes her eyes for a moment. *What, then, are we to do?* No answers come. Only an image: a hillside brown as a lion's skin, her husband running with a spool, her son yelling his excitement as she releases the kite. The fabric unfurling above them into the brief, vivid shape of human joy.

THE FORGOTTEN CHILDREN

THROUGH THE YEARS of my childhood when there wasn't much else to hold on to, I had a fantasy. Those rum-scented evenings when Father's slurred yells slammed into the peeling walls of wherever we were living at the moment, I would lie wedged behind a sofa or under a bed, and close my eyes and slide into it. Sometimes my brother lay there also, curled tight against me, sucking his thumb, although Mother had told him he was too old to be doing that. The knobs of his spine would push into my chest; his heart would thud against my palm like the hooves of a runaway horse—like my own heart, so that after a while I couldn't tell the two apart. Maybe that's how he, too, became part of the fantasy.

Our family moved a lot those days, flurried migrations that took us from rooming house to dingier rooming house as my father lost one job after another. He always managed to find a new one because he was a skilled machinist—perhaps that was part of his trouble, knowing that he would. But each job was a little worse than the previous one, a small movement down the spiral that our life had turned into. We never spoke of it—we were not a family much given to discussion. But we saw it in our mother's face, the way she sometimes broke off in the middle of a sentence and stared out the window, forgetting that my brother and I were waiting.

We children learned some skills of our own as we traveled through the small hot factory towns of north India that after a while blurred into a single oily smell, a grimy dust that stung the nostrils. We knew how to be almost invisible as we sat on the last bench in class, not knowing the answers because we had missed the previous lessons or didn't have the books. Or as we sat in the far corner of the canteen at lunchtime because we didn't want anyone to see the rolled brown rutis Mother packed for us in old paper. We looked longingly—but sidewise, so no one would guess—at the starched uniforms of the others, their tiffin boxes filled with sandwiches made from store-bought bread so white it dazzled the eye. Each time they laughed, we flinched, pulling the edge of a skirt over a bruised thigh, a shirtsleeve over discolored finger marks left on a forearm. Were they talking about us—how Mother had asked the sabji-wallah for credit, how Father had to be helped home from the toddy shop last payday? How long before they learned of the noises that sometimes exploded from our flat at night? We learned to arrange our hair so that the pink ridges of a forehead scar would hardly show. To look casually into the middle distance, as though we didn't notice the curious eyes. To not think of the futile, scattered trailings we had left behind: a book of fairy tales, a stray yellow dog we used to feed, a mango tree perfect for climbing, the few friendships formed before we knew better.

We. That was how I thought of my brother in those days, as though he were as much a part of me as my arm or leg. Indispensable, to be protected instinctively, like one shields the face from a blow, but not something one thinks about. It never occurred to me as he followed me around in silence (he was not a talkative boy) that he might feel differently about our life—that knotted, misshapen thing, like a fracture healed wrong—which I accepted because it was what I'd always known. Perhaps that was my first mistake.

The year I was eleven and my brother eight, we ended

up in Duligarh, an Assam oil town as sagging and discolored as a cardboard box left to rot in the rain. It was a town of many toddy shops, all of which my father would soon discover. A town where credit was difficult to get, where from the first people looked at us with faces like closed fists. I didn't blame them. We were a far cry from the model families displayed on the family-planning posters the municipal office had put up all over town.

One of these posters was pasted on the back wall of our school. I remember it perfectly from all the afternoons I stood there looking up until my neck ached. My fantasy fed on that poster through those sweat-studded afternoons, spreading its insidious roots, leading me to my other errors.

In the poster, a young couple held hands and smiled into each other's eyes while a boy and girl played tag around them. The man carried a shiny leather briefcase. The woman's gold chain sparkled in the sun, and the edge of her pink sari lifted in the breeze. The children wore real leather Bata shoes, the kind I'd seen in the store window in Lal Bahadur Market, spit-shined to a mirror polish. *We Two, Our Two*, declared the poster, as though it were the mantra for a happy life. *We Two, Our Two*. Where then had our parents gone wrong?

Sometimes I stood watching until the sky changed to the dull yellow of late afternoon and my brother tugged at my arm in exasperation. Let's go, Didi, I'm hungry. Why do you like to waste your time staring at that silly picture? He wanted, instead, to be shaking down ripe guavas from the trees on the edge of the orchard across the street. People shouldn't plant their trees along the public road if they don't want anyone to pick the fruit, he said, thrusting out his chin, when I protested.

Sometimes we missed the bus because of that poster and had to walk home, trudging through the heat, our clothes sticking to our skin, our books getting heavier, all the way past the edge of town. Walking through the bazaar I would feel the shopkeepers' unsmiling eyes on us, a lanky girl with hair pulled back in two tight, careful braids, a juice-stained boy with his wrists sticking out of a shirt he'd outgrown, striding impatiently ahead of his sister. Did they connect us with our parents—that woman who came down to the bazaar at the end of the day, moving among the dull-scaled fish and shriveled beans, her beautiful face like a parched oleander, that man who held his body with brilliant belligerence like a boxer who knew that the key to his survival was to trust no one? Did they compare us to the family on the poster?

IN ASSAM WE lived in an old British bungalow which we children loved. It was the first real house we'd lived in, a long, low structure built for some forgotten purpose outside of town. It was inconveniently far from everything (it took Father an hour to bike to the factory where he tested drilling equipment), but the rent was cheap and there were no prying neighbors. If it was lonely for Mother all day when we were gone, she didn't complain. Perhaps she was glad to have the time to herself. Only occasionally would she grumble that the house was falling apart on us.

And it was. Perhaps in sympathy with some other, invisible disintegration, flakes of falling plaster coated everything like giant dandruff. The windows would not shut properly, so that malevolent-looking insects with burnished stings wandered in at will. The roof leaked and when it rained, which was often, we had to make our way around strategically placed buckets.

But we children thought it was perfect—the wooden porch where we played marbles, the claw-footed bathtub where Mother would pour steaming water for our baths, the spear-shaped grilles at the windows that made us feel as if we were living in a medieval fortress.

Best of all we loved the servant's quarter, a small cottage set far back into the bamboo grove that grew behind the house. My brother and I were the first to discover it. When we told Mother, she gave an unusually bitter laugh. A servant's quarter for us! she said, the corners of her mouth turning downward. What a joke! For a while she kept asking Father to see if he could rent it out to one of the factory watchmen. But nothing ever came of that. Perhaps we were too far from the factory. Perhaps Father, who wasn't the type to go around asking, never mentioned it to anyone. My brother believed it was because he and I had prayed so hard for it to stay empty.

The cottage was dim and cool even in the brassy Assam afternoons because it sat under a huge tree of a kind I'd never seen before, with large round leaves like upturned palms. Spiderwebs hung from its ceilings, intelligently angled to enmesh intruders, and in the far room we discovered a trapdoor that blended almost perfectly into the wooden flooring. Underneath was a small space with a packed dirt floor, just right for a make-believe prison or an underground cave. We told no one of it, and never used it ourselves. It was enough to know it was there. Instead, we dusted off a rope cot that was in the corner and dragged it over the trapdoor to hide it. Then we smuggled an old sheet from the house. In the afternoons when we got back from school we lay on the cot in the half-dark and I told my brother stories.

That was when I told my brother about the fantasy. For a long time I'd kept it to myself, knowing instinctively that it was not for sharing. But something about the cottage made me feel weightless and uncatchable, as though I were a dust mote tumbling in lazy light. When I looked up from the cot, the leaves made a canopy of hands, holding off the rest of my life. I'd thought my pragmatic brother would laugh at the fantasy. But from the beginning it was his favorite, the final story I had to tell before we returned to the house to help Mother with chores.

HERE IS THE fantasy:

My parents are moving again. They climb into a battered three-wheeler loaded down with bundles and boxes. But we are not with them because they have forgotten us. From behind the bamboo grove we watch as the three-wheeler lurches to a start, as it becomes smaller and smaller and finally disappears. We emerge from the fronds cautiously. Yes, they're really gone. For a moment we are stunned. Then we grab each other and spin until the world is an ecstatic whirl.

The fantasy is not without its problems. The most important one is our mother. Just before she gets into the three-wheeler she looks around uncertainly, the way an animal might, scenting something amiss in the air. (I do not tell my brother this, but I know he sees it, too.) I would like to include her in the fantasy. To have her see a flicker of white—my brother's shirt—in the bamboo. She would walk into the grove to explore and never return to my father. But I know it cannot be. Their lives are tangled together beyond my powers of extrication. So, sadly, I let her go.

We live in the servant's quarter. By now the bamboo has grown so thick that no one remembers the existence of the cottage. I cook and clean and teach my brother everything I learned at school. He catches fish for us in the stream behind the cottage, lots of fish, and we sell some of it in the bazaar and buy rice, salt, shoes. We begin to look like the children in the family-planning poster.

You think I'll be able to catch that many? my brother always asks at this point, not totally convinced of his angling skills.

Of course, I reply.

In our fantasy, no one drags us over the cracked driveway so that its exposed brick scours our backs. In the dark garage, no one lights a match and brings it so close that we can feel the heat of it on our eyelids. In our fantasy, entire sections of words have disappeared from the dictionary: *fear, fracture, furious, fatal, father.*

We keep on living like this.

What about when we get old? my brother asks.

We don't, I say. But he is not satisfied. So I have to devise an end for the fantasy.

One winter it snows and snows.

Snow? asks my brother. He has never seen any. Nor have I, but in my geography book I've come across pictures of the silvered peaks of the Himalayas. I explain it to him.

One winter it snows and snows. The snow drifts in through the windows and doors. It falls on the bed where the brother and sister are sleeping side by side.

Like this? My brother slips his hand into mine and lays his head on my shoulder. A pale scar whose origin I cannot remember slants across his cheekbone.

Yes, I say.

The snow forms a thick white quilt that covers the brother and sister. It doesn't hurt. They never wake up. They sleep like this forever.

Sleep forever, repeats my brother consideringly as we walk back to the house through the humid afternoon.

THINGS WERE DISAPPEARING from the house. At first it was food, little items that Mother wouldn't have noticed if money hadn't been so tight—a small box of biscuits, a half-empty packet of sugar. Then it was clothes—an old shirt of my brother's, my green kameez with the frayed collar. A moth-eaten blanket that Mother was intending to throw away as soon as we could afford a new one.

Did you take it for a game? she asked when I came into the kitchen for a snack after school.

No, I didn't, I said, glad not to have to lie. I was afraid she might follow up with questions I'd have more difficulty sidestepping. But she shook her head in a preoccupied way and started kneading dough for rutis.

I can't figure it out, she said. It's not as though we have a servant who might be stealing. And now the level in the rice bin seems to be dropping.

Spirits, that's what it is, declared Lakshmi-aunty, the old woman who sold spices down in the bazaar, when Mother mentioned it to her the next day. Spirits. People say a saheb lived in that house a long time ago—a smuggler, they say he was—came to a bad end. Hanged himself from the living room rafters. Here, take this mustard seed and burn it in an iron pot while chanting the name of Rama. That should make the spirit go away.

The next afternoon when we returned from school, Mother did as Lakshmi-aunty had instructed. We helped her with the homemade exorcism, chanting and sneezing as the acrid smoke rose from the pot and the mustard seeds began to sputter. We said nothing to Father.

For a while after that, there were no more disappearances. By the time they started again, Mother had worse problems to worry about.

———————

FATHER HAD FALLEN foul of the foreman. It wasn't unexpected. At each of his jobs he found someone to hate, someone who, he believed, was out to get him. (Why does he always have to fight with people? my brother asked once. Mother sighed and said he always was a free spirit, he never did take kindly to being ordered around.) It was only a matter of time before the chance remark exploded into a fistfight or worse. In the last town he'd gashed an overseer's arm with a broken bottle, and the police had taken him away for a while. Then we would be packing again, looking up railway timetables, deciding what to leave behind.

At dinner Father ate sullenly, muttering curses at the foreman, not noticing what kind of food Mother put in front of him. He held tightly to the neck of a bottle, raised it to his mouth in one glinting arc. Mother would rub his arm, a gesture which sometimes calmed him. From the table in the corner where we did our homework, we could see the muscles of her back through the thin fabric of her blouse, bunched with tension. Just try to avoid him, please, she'd whisper. Why don't you ask for a transfer to another shift? Think of the children—they're just beginning to settle down, to catch up in school. Times are so bad, what if you don't find another job. You're not getting any younger either. . . .

Some nights he would merely shake his head and say, You're right, Mother, that whoremonger isn't worth the spit out of my mouth. Or he would swat her entreating hands away, growling, Leave me alone, woman, don't interfere in things you know nothing about. But there were those other nights. Bitch, we'd hear him bellow, and we'd melt into the moldy shadows under the porch. Here I am, killing myself to feed all of you, and all you do is nag at me. Sound of a slap, a pan clanking onto the floor, spilling the dal that was to have been our lunch tomorrow. A breathless grunt. We knew how it felt, that fist slammed into the side of the head, turning everything black for a moment. The kick against the ribs that left you knotted and gasping on the floor. And the pain. We knew about pain. How it rose like a wall of water and crashed over you. We gripped each other's hands, afraid even to sob, hating ourselves for not trying to stop him. We held our breath and plunged into our other fantasy, the one we shared without ever having spoken it, where our father was dead, dead, dead.

I never asked Mother why she didn't leave him, though I often wondered. Why didn't she run away with us to her parents' village? She sometimes described it wistfully as a peaceful cluster of huts under emerald coconut trees filled with singing birds. (I didn't know then that she had eloped with Father and, in the traditional Indian scheme of things, had shut that door behind herself forever.) Was it that she feared Father was just too powerful? That wherever we went, he would smell us out, like the ogre in a fairy tale?

No. There was something else, which I couldn't quite put into words. It had to do with my father's broad shoulders, the muscles that rippled along his arms like playful snakes when he swung us up. The way he could make us feel safe even when we were high in the air. The way he could make us forget. Maybe it was the sun woven into his thick black hair, the fresh smell of ritha in it on holidays after Mother had washed it for him. He'd burst into snatches of song (he had once taken lessons, Mother said), his voice rising as unhesitant as light—*Mehbooba, Mehbooba, my dearest darling*—until it came up against the words he had forgotten. Then he'd throw himself at Mother's feet like a hero out of a Hindi movie, arms flung out, until she couldn't stop herself from laughing. Or he would come home with a package tied with the flat red string used by sari shops. He would gather her to him and thrust it into her hands. And while her trembling fingers tugged at the knots and a blush rose up from her throat (my mother was unusually fair, with skin that bruised easily), he would drop a kiss on the top of her head or play with the ends of her long braid.

Once when I woke late at night and went to the kitchen for a tumbler of water, I found them sitting at the table, their backs toward me. Perhaps it was one of those times when the electric company had cut off our power because we couldn't pay, for there was a small kerosene lamp on the table between them.

Shanti, my father was saying in a small, choked voice, I've only made you unhappy. Sometimes I wish we'd never met. Or that I were dead. On the wall his shadow hunkered, anguished, against her slim silhouette. My very own Beauty and the Beast. Mother put her hand over his mouth, and her voice, too, was choked. Hush, Swapan (it was the first time I heard her call him by his name), don't say that. How could I live on without you?

I tried to back away silently, but Father saw me. I couldn't breathe. He would be furious now. I'd spoiled it all. But he held out an arm, and when I edged over, he sat me on his lap and stroked my hair. His hand was awkward with the unaccustomed motion and his calluses caught in my hair, but I didn't want him to stop. Mother leaned her head against his shoulder. The planes of her face were angular and lovely in the flickering light. Her eyes were tightly shut, as though in prayer. I breathed in their blended odor—his Teen Patti tobacco, her sweet Neem soap—and in that way I came to know something of love, how complex it is, how filled with the need to believe.

WE CAME HOME from school and the black trunk was in our bedroom. Its lid was open and some of our clothes had already been thrown inside. They formed small wadded lumps at the bottom of the box. When I looked at them, I wanted to cry.

We went to find Mother, who was in the kitchen emptying the rickety wire cabinet where she kept the spices.

We're leaving day after tomorrow, she said. She didn't offer any explanation and we didn't ask. There were new lines at the corners of her eyes and mouth, as though someone had lifted the skin off her face, crumpled it, and then replaced it carelessly. We went back to our room, and I emptied out the trunk to pack it right, shoes and books at the bottom, clothes on top, folded into neat squares, like I knew from all those other times.

Come and help me, I said to my brother, but he lay on his mattress and stared at the cracks in the ceiling until it grew dark and the cicadas outside started their buzzing. He spoke only once, when I tried to pack his clothes. Don't touch my things, he said. His voice was decisive in its viciousness, like a grownup's.

When I woke in the morning, he was gone.

WHERE IS HE? Father yelled again. Spittle from his mouth struck my cheek and I flinched, though I tried not to.

Leave the poor girl alone. Mother's voice rose up from behind, startling me with its brittle, unusual loudness. Her hair, come undone from its neat knot, hung wild about her face, and her sari was splotched with mud from the ditch behind the house where she'd been searching, calling my brother's name. There was an unmoored look in her eyes. She's been telling you all day that she doesn't know. Why don't you bike down instead to the bus station in the bazaar and ask if anyone saw him?

I drew in a sharp breath and stiffened in readiness, but perhaps Father was as taken aback as I was. He got on his cycle and left.

Once my father's silhouette, wavery black against the setting sun, disappeared around the bend, Mother slumped down on the kitchen floor. She did this jerkily, in stages, as if a series of springs inside her were snapping, one by one. Surrounded by the cheap aluminum pots and chipped dishes that summarized her life, she put her face in her hands and began to cry. It was a sound like cloth tearing. Not even the time when she had to go to the clinic to have her arm set had she cried like this. I went and put my arms around her. My chest felt as though it was tearing, too. I almost told her then.

Mother looked up as though she could sense my thoughts. She wasn't crying anymore.

You know where he is, don't you, she said. She caught

me by the elbows. Please tell me, please. Her voice sounded as though it were pushing its way past something that had broken and stuck in her throat. I promise I won't let your father do anything to him.

I bit down on my lips because I didn't want to hurt her further. But I couldn't stop myself. You always did before, I said. What's so different about this time?

Something passed over Mother's face. Was it sorrow, or a cloud of shame? She took a deep breath, as though preparing for an underwater journey, then cupped my face in her hands. Her nails were broken and dirt-caked, but her fingers were long and cool. I'll protect my baby, she said quietly. I swear it on my dead mother's soul.

I believed her then, although she hadn't answered my question. Perhaps it was because she wasn't a woman who promised lightly. Or because her face was so like my brother's with those same straight eyebrows, the same scattering of moles across the cheekbones. The face I loved most in all the world, after his. Or because finally, with the tarry night pressing itself down on us, I accepted what I'd always known in some vanquished part of myself: Fantasies can't really come true.

HE WAS WHERE I thought he would be, huddled against the far corner of the crawl space my parents had missed in their perfunctory search of the servant's quarter. (They hadn't believed he would choose such an obvious place, so close to home, to hide in.) When I pushed away the cot and lifted the trapdoor, his eyes glinted, feral, in the beam from Mother's flashlight. There were crumbs around his mouth from the biscuits he'd been eating. Around his shoulders was bunched the old blanket he'd secreted away a long time back, believing in imagination. I reached down to help him up, but he shrank from me, his face heavy with hate.

MOTHER CARRIED MY brother all the way back to the house, although he was really too heavy for her, holding him close to her chest as one would an infant. She asked me to walk ahead with the flashlight, so I didn't hear what she was murmuring to him, but by the time they were in the kitchen, he had stopped struggling. He even managed a small smile when Mother fixed us mashed rice and bananas with hot milk and sugar, which used to be his favorite meal when he was little.

We had just started eating when we heard Father. He made his way up the porch slowly and noisily, and once it sounded like he bumped into the wall. We froze, my brother and I at the table, the food halfway to our mouths, Mother at the counter where she had been chopping bananas. Then he was in the kitchen, the kicked-open door banging against the wall, the hulk of his shadow falling on the table between my brother and me. His huge voice filled me, the echoes booming outward until I thought I would split open.

I remember the rest only in fragments, black-and-white frames that appear even now without warning, branding themselves across my vision, forcing me to abandon whatever I'm doing. I'm going to kill you today, you little shit-eater. Heavy clunk of a belt being unbuckled. My brother runs for my mother. She must have thrust him behind her, because he's gone and instead I see her hands, the fingers stiffly splayed, pushing against Father's chest. Her mouth's open, she's shouting something, she's on the floor. The belt moves through the air in a perfect, lazy arc. Now it's a cobra, striking, the metal fang gashing my brother's cheek just under his left eye, gouging out a piece of flesh, the blood exploding from what is left. A thin scream that goes on and on. Mother you promised you promised you . . . She pushes me out of her way, grasps the edge of the counter to pull herself up. Her hand closes around the knife. And now the voice is screaming again. I listen. I have no control over the voice, which I recognize vaguely as my own. Father turns. The belt buckle catches mother's wrist. A crack, as of a stick snapping. I hear the knife clatter down, each metallic unit of sound clear and disparate. A sound, half whinny, half gasp, reeling back into itself. They must both be on the floor, grappling for it.

But I can't tell what's going on back there because I've turned to watch my brother, who is running, who has made it through the door and past the porch and out to the bamboo grove. The sheltering dark gathers him in—elbows and knees, hands, the back of his head. Only his shirt glows in the moonlight like the snow we had imagined together, then disappears as he steps into shadow, then glows more palely farther ahead. There are fireflies everywhere tonight, pinpoints of light blurring into a luminous ooze. Perhaps to disappear is the next best thing to being forgotten. Am I crying from happiness because he has escaped, if only for now? Or is it regret at that thin scream (my final error?) which shot from my mouth like an arrow of blood? Is it because I know I cannot join him? That in a moment I (my mother's daughter, bound after all by her genes of mistimed loyalties) must turn toward whatever is behind me, wheezing wetly, trying to get to its feet? All I know is that this is how I will remember my brother: a patch of dwindling white (melting, melting) as the bamboos shiver close. As the fireflies hover above him with their frail, fitful light.

THE BLOOMING SEASON
FOR CACTI

TO GET TO California I had to travel through desert. But, no, the desert was part of California, too. Perhaps the best part, I would think later. Brown land, brown sky, hills like brown breasts. The Greyhound bus fishtailed in the wind, or maybe the driver was sleepy. I slid across the worn-slick vinyl seat with a slash in its center, as if someone had had to hide something fast. Or maybe he'd been searching. Or merely bored and needed it, the hard defined sound of the rip as the knife bit in, its controlled movement across the drab olive flatness. I slid all the way across and hit my head against the dusty window, but it didn't hurt because I'd seen it coming and braced myself. Oh, I was quick. Because only the quick survive. Or the fortunate—but already my life had proved I wasn't that.

We were passing the dunes now, the sand rippled into a thousand lines of cursive, a dangerous alphabet. Everywhere, mica glittered like eyes. Above, vultures waited to swoop down on the helpless skitter of smaller creatures. I loved it—how could I resist? I wanted to climb to the top of the highest dune. I wanted to be transformed to the bone.

Some of the scared hardness at my core was melting in the desert's heat. For the first time since I got to America.

I felt myself growing into all the words my sister-in-law had shouted as I packed my things in her Dallas home two days ago. Selfish, yes. Ungrateful, yes. Following only my own pleasure. I would be all that.

I was a burning wind. I was a lit fuse.

And I was coming to California.

BUT FIRST THERE was the lush, sweaty jostle of Bombay, the torrential monsoons that swept through the city where I was born, the greedy, flooded streets that sucked at your calves. On each corner the looming billboards promised romance, a dark air-conditioned theater and Amir Khan in your arms—or Madhuri Dixit, depending on your preference. All the passion you could want and none of the consequences. The white ocean at night, necklaced with lights from Marine Drive, rocked just for you.

Everything I had loved, and then hated.

People thought I came to Texas because my older brother was the only relative I had left. The real reason was that I needed something as different as possible from Bombay. How else could I begin to bear the memories, the city smoldering in the aftermath of riot? Hindus and Muslims, that inexplicable frenzy, smoke that rose solid in a hundred pillars. On the street, screams of women whose accents you could not have distinguished from mine. The smell of the water tank on our terrace where my mother made me hide.

What did I imagine? Open country, dust rising from hooves as herds headed home. Fountains of iridescent oil. Cougars. Cowboys with creased smiles and eyes blue as sapphire stone. Their kisses would be hard and innocent. Behind us in the night, rockets would take off for the moon, searing a path brighter than any meteor.

I found myself in a two-bedroom semidetached exactly like a hundred others, a pocket-sized square of lawn, browning in patches because water cost too much. "We'll put in rocks, once we're sure your brother won't get laid off," said my sister-in-law, who was kind in the beginning. "Come on, Mira, let's take you to the mall."

It was my own fault, my desperate mythologizing of America. But I blamed her for my disappointment. And my brother. I blamed him for his patience, his second-rate career, his crumpled, apologetic shoulders. His letter which had asked me to come stay with him. *It's not safe in India, how many times I told you and Mother this. More so now that you're unmarried and alone.*

The bus jerks to a halt. How many hours? It is a gray afternoon, a gray wind blowing Burger King wrappers across a scraggly city park. Gulls circle overhead, screaming, though there is no sign of water. I see graffiti on peeling walls, metal bars in a shop window.

"Sacramento," shouts the driver, and I climb down.

IT IS DUSK by the time I find Malik's restaurant. The light has seeped away, leaving ink pools under the eyes of strangers in the street, in the secretive hollows of their throat.

In Bombay, before the riots, darkness had fallen dramatically, in one gay swoop.

Comparisons are futile, I know that. Now is all I have. But my feet hurt, the backpack straps bite into my shoulders, and the *frr-frr* of pigeons flying home is the rustle of my mother's sari.

"Malik-ji?" says the manager, who is at the cash register, picking his teeth. "Yes, he's in. You're lucky. He hardly ever comes into the restaurant anymore." He peers at the note which my brother had insisted on giving me. "I don't know if he'll talk to you. So many people come through here, claiming to be relatives of relatives."

The air is cumin and coriander, a roasted brown smell. They must be frying samosas inside. My mother used to make the best samosas, fat and crisp. "Stuff carefully, Mira," she'd say. "Wet the dough ends and pinch the tips together so no air bubbles remain." But I never had the patience.

"Did I say I was a relative?" I let my voice hit the shadowed ceiling. My head feels like a bubble, enormous with hot air. "I'm looking for a job. If you don't have one, I'll be happy to look elsewhere."

A few early diners turn to stare.

"Arre bas, what temper," says the manager, not unkindly. "Just left home, didn't you? A week on the streets and you'd be singing a different song. Sit there, on the empty side, I'll go ask if he'll see you. Ei Priya, bring this bahinji a cup of chai."

I sit in the banquet section of the restaurant, decorated

with maroon velvet and mirrors, curtains with thick gold pull ropes, wall-to-wall plush carpeting. I want to feel disdain. In our drawing room in Bombay there had been a hundred-year-old rug from Srinagar that belonged to my grandfather, its faded design a glimmering of jewels through fog. But this American carpet is so soft around my ankles, so innocent of history—like young grass—that I can't stop myself from slipping off my shoes.

The tea comes, brought by a young woman in a purple sari and neat braids. Her blackbird eyes take in my wrinkled jeans, my less-than-clean shirt, my hair bundled into a knot, even—I am sure—the giant blister taking angry shape on my left heel. She is about to speak, but someone shouts "Pri-ya," and with a flash of a smile she is gone. The kitchen door swings open to her touch, closes on a burst of female laughter, a question that could be *Who is she*, or maybe *What does she want*, the old, known smells and the boundaries they once promised. Sputtering mustard seed, the bright green glaze of chilies cooking in my mother's karhai. I no longer feel desert-dangerous, only tired and, again, afraid.

THE WATER TANK in our Bombay house smelled of river bottoms, of rust, of sun-heated metal and still water. Inside, it was colder than I had expected, shiver-cold, and the smallest sounds echoed and boomed against my ear.

We were lucky to have a water tank at all. It had been put in a long time ago by my grandfather, when such things were still allowed. Having grown up in the lake-filled villages of Bengal, he had liked long baths. Now it meant that when the municipal supply was cut off twice a day, we had water to cook and drink.

But our real luck lay in the fact that none of the surrounding houses had tanks. This meant the rioters would not think to look on the terrace, my mother said. From her voice I knew she was only hoping.

The tank was not large. Still, it could have held us both. When I said that, my mother shook her head. "I must padlock the house from outside," she said. "That way they might believe it's empty."

"Where will you go?" I asked.

"I've let half the tank water out," she said, "but you might need the rest. It's a good thing this old lid doesn't close too well. There'll be enough air. Don't come out, no matter what you hear. Here's some fruit, it's the only thing that'll keep in there. Eat it sparingly. Who knows when—"

There were shouts in the distance, a rumbling sound like heavy machinery. Perhaps there were guns. I thought I smelled burning oil.

My mother pushed me down into the tank, handed me a banana and two oranges. She let her hand linger for a moment on my hair. "God bless you," she said.

I thought of saying, *Who? The god that's letting this happen to us, to this city?* And, *What if they set the house on fire?* Of saying, *None of this would have happened if we'd moved to America after Baba died, like my brother invited us to.*

If there's one thing I'm glad of now, it's that I stayed silent.

I ate the banana that night. Next evening I ate the oranges. The screams had stopped by then, mostly. I let the peels fall from my hand and watched them float, slow motion, to the tank bottom. I crushed the seeds in my teeth as though the bitterness could bring me relief. For a long time, the moist, weighted air of the tank smelled of oranges and tears.

"YOU WON'T BE happy working for me, not for long," says Malik in his resigned, matter-of-fact voice. "You're too educated, too smart, I can see it in your face. . . ."

What had I expected him to look like? When my brother told me of his empire of restaurants and groceries and apartment buildings, I'd pictured someone like Seth

Ramchand back home, corpulent in an overstarched Nehru jacket, smoking a cheroot, flashing a diamond on every finger. Or, given the American context, maybe a suave, Armani-clad villain. (Who but a villain could so easily rake in the millions that steadily eluded my brother?) Body-guards would hover in the background as he stepped out, dark-glassed, from his limousine. But here he is, a trim man, not too tall, with a bland blue department-store shirt and a cautious haircut. (He does own a limousine, but I will not learn this fact until much later.) His mustache is neat and nondescript. I've seen a thousand mustaches like that on the streets of Bombay.

"Too pretty also," says Malik, and suddenly the look in his eyes is neither bland nor cautious.

WHEN I ANNOUNCED my plans for leaving Dallas, my brother tried his best to stop me. He explained how dan-gerous it was, a girl traveling America alone. *Dangerous* was a word my brother liked to use. In this he was like all men who have never experienced its reality firsthand. He cajoled and pleaded, said he'd pay for me to take classes at the local community college. He tried damage containment. "Why does it have to be California? Go to the East Coast instead, if it's excitement you want. I have friends in New

Jersey, solid family men, they'll take you in, treat you like a sister."

At last he gave me Malik's address in Sacramento. He and my brother had gone to college together briefly, before Malik dropped out to start his first restaurant. Now they stayed desultorily in touch, sending each other Diwali cards, informing each other of the births of children or changes of address.

My brother kept at me until I said, Very well, I would go to Sacramento rather than Los Angeles, like I wanted. Even then he wasn't happy.

"Leaving us like this to live by yourself," he said at the bus station, handing me my backpack with a sigh. "Ma would have been most upset! Oh, well, at least Malik will be there in case you run into trouble. But you'd better . . ."

I'd shoved past him without answering. My face felt like someone had rubbed ground glass into it. What right did he have to speak of my mother? He wasn't the one who'd searched for her through streets filled with the stench of kerosene and burned flesh, calling her name. He wasn't the one who had gone to one police station after another with her photo, to be told by exhausted officials that there were too many missing people for them to keep track.

"Maybe it's better if you don't find her," one inspector had told me finally.

I kept my face turned away from the tinted bus window, from my brother's waving arm, the crease of worry between his brows, simple as a Crayola line drawn by a child. Still, I heard him through the engine's backfiring: "... watch out for Malik—he has a reputation."

I SIT ON one end of the sagging sofa that takes up most of our living room and watch Priya trying on makeup. She outlines her lips in Scarlet Madness and pouts into the mirror she is holding. She flutters her mascara-thickened lashes. She is practicing, because soon she is to be a wife. Her hair, unbraided now, falls over her left breast.

Malik has given me a job at the restaurant—I am to be a cashier, morning shift, until I'm ready to handle the heavier evening crowds—and a room in an apartment building he owns down the street. The rent, to be deducted from my pay, is reasonable. I can eat in the restaurant kitchen for free, if I wish.

"He's a fair man, you have to admit," Priya says as she shifts her hips, trying to find a comfortable spot on the sofa. She wears a demure nightgown, high-necked and long-sleeved. Malik had called her into his office and told her that he was putting me in her apartment, since it had a second bedroom. I would have resented the intrusion, but she doesn't seem to mind. "Also kind. Looking at him, you'd never believe the stories."

She pauses, lips parted expectantly, until I ask what the stories are.

I listen absently as she talks of under-the-table deals with warehouses, a partner who died too conveniently, huge bribes paid to Immigration so they won't look too closely at his employees' visas. A manager who crossed him, and now he's gone, disappeared, even his family doesn't know where. And then there's the matter of his second wife.

Priya's sleeves are pulled up above her elbow, her arms are smooth and dimpled as she raises them in a languorous stretch. She undoes the two top buttons of her gown—it is a warm night—and fans herself with an old copy of *Good Housekeeping*. The damp gleam of her skin disturbs me. But why? Where I come from, it isn't unusual for women to undress in front of each other. Growing up, I saw naked women many times, in the jenana changing rooms by the sea, and paid them no more attention than the rickety clothes racks on which we threw our saris.

"He saw her on a trip back to India—by chance, just like in the movies! He'd gone to his cousin's village for a wedding, and saw her in the crowd of guests. He liked her so much he married her that same week, didn't even ask for a dowry. Her parents were delighted, they knew how rich he was. But when she got here she found he was married already, even had kids and all. So she tried to kill herself. Slit her wrists, right here in this building—he'd put her on the top floor, in the best apartment. What a mess it was, ambulances, police, scared us all to death."

A lot of women killed themselves after the Bombay riots. People were shocked, but not surprised. *For centuries of Indian women*, the editor of a Hindu newspaper wrote, *it has been the honorable way. Remember Queen Padmini of olden times, who, along with her attendant women, threw herself into the fire rather than become her Muslim captor's concubine?*

In modern Bombay, death by hanging, a noose made from a sari, was the most common. Those who had connections and money bought sleeping pills. A few women swam out into the ocean.

"She didn't die," Priya says, "luckily." Her voice wavers over the word, unsure if it's the right one. "Malik-ji must have felt terribly guilty, because he transferred the building to her name, yes, the whole thing, she owns it all, they say it's worth a million and a half, maybe more. I think he really loves her, but of course he can't divorce his first wife because of the children. Every Friday night he sends his limousine for her—oh, you must see it, I've heard it even has a TV and a fridge inside. And she'll come down the steps in a silk sari and diamonds, with tuberoses in her hair, beautiful, but in a sad kind of way, like Jaya Bhaduri in *Silsila*, you remember? When she finds out that Amitabh has been having an affair with Rekha? You'll see when you meet her. . . ."

My mother used to wear tuberoses. After my father died, she gave up the habit as a vanity. But she would place bowls of the slim, fragrant flowers on tables and windowsills, so that a visitor, coming in from the bustle of the city, would be faced with cool whiteness. When I allow myself to think of it, I like to believe that she was one of the women who swam out to sea.

"Just two more months left," Priya says as she begins to wipe off her makeup, "for my wedding. He's in India. My parents have set everything up. I've been saving all my money for the trousseau."

My mother would have swum through the warm salt—we had done it many times together—her sari growing heavy with it. Maybe she would have loosened the cloth and let it drift from her so she could move more freely. The waves were silver, like flying fish. They bore her up, they sang in her ear. Behind her the charred mass of the city drifted away, terror and loss. Did she look back in the direction of our house?

"How about you?" asks Priya. "What are you saving for?"

I don't reply.

"Never mind," says Priya kindly, patting my shoulder. Her lips glisten like wet plums. "Things will work out. You're so pretty, you're sure to find a husband soon."

THE TROUBLE STARTED about a month after I arrived in Dallas, in my sister-in-law's house. But there were signs earlier. Hushed consultations in the corners of parties, telephone conversations that turned innocuous when I entered the room. Appraising glances. Little questions here and there, sharp as ant bites.

"Mira, dear, what did you think of Mr. Advani, the man in the maroon Adidas T-shirt who brought us drinks—most attentive, wasn't he?"

"Don't you just love Ashok's jokes, Mira? The one about the sardarji today—oh, I laughed so much I thought I would burst."

"He was most attentive," I would say. "That joke was hilarious." Then I would go to my room.

On this day, just as we started dinner, my sister-in-law

said, "Mira, you'll never guess what happened this afternoon. Arpan Basu called your brother at work. He wants to marry you!"

She waited for excitement, delight, coy confusion at the very least—Arpan was eminently eligible; he owned his own company, something to do with bathroom cleaners.

"I don't want to get married," I said.

"Why not?" asked my sister-in-law. "So he has a slight receding-hairline problem. What does that matter when he's so enthusiastic about the match?"

I didn't reply.

"What, you think you're too good for him, for all our friends?"

"Please—" said my brother.

"Ask your sister," said my sister-in-law to my brother, "if she doesn't want to get married, what *does* she want? Now if she had a brilliant career, instead a job selling pots and pans at Sears—"

"Please," said my brother, putting his hand on her arm. "Don't you remember how it was for you when you first came here? Mira's been through a lot. She needs time."

My sister-in-law bit her lip and was silent. When she spoke again, her voice was different. For just a moment it made me see that all our lives have depths which strangers can never chart. And that's what we were to each other, strangers.

"Unfortunately," she said, "time doesn't wait for women to recover. Today the men are buzzing around Mira. Tomorrow, who knows?"

I watched them sitting across the table from me, a graying man, a woman tending toward plumpness. They meant well. How could I tell them that when I thought of a man touching me, I smelled the water tank: smoke and corroding metal. Below, the streets were filled with weeping, struggling women, their blouses ripped open, their bodies pinned down right there, on the pavement's dirt. The mob yelling encouragement.

"A marriage might help her get over what happened," my sister-in-law said.

THAT NIGHT IN my room in my brother's house I took down the atlas of the United States, opened it to the word that gleamed at the edge of the continent. *California.*

My mother and I had discussed California after my father's death, when we received the first of my brother's letters asking us to come stay with him. He included postcards from a trip they'd taken to Los Angeles: Hollywood, Universal Studios, a boardwalk somewhere with Ferris wheels against an unnaturally brilliant ocean. One particular card, titled *Mojave*, was all glinting rock and cactus.

"If I were a traveling kind of woman," my mother had said, "I'd go one time, just to see California. They say there's still gold in the deserts there. They say the beaches are more beautiful than ours in Bombay."

We'd caught each other's eye and laughed disbelievingly. Gold in desert sand? Beaches more beautiful than Bombay's?

Now I closed the atlas and sank back against my pillow, its small comfort. Small comforts were all I had: a softness beneath my head, a place to go next.

All night as I slept for the last time in my brother's house, California was the brightness that pulsed through the contracting chambers of my heart.

THE MORNING AFTER Priya has told me her story, I see Malik's second wife. I am about to go for a walk. She is emptying an apartment someone has moved out of, trying to pull a broken armchair through the doorway.

The sun is not yet up. The breeze is still cool. A hint of cloud floats like lace in the sky. Dressed in old sweats, a smudge of dust on her cheek, she is older than I am. By how much I can't tell. Is she beautiful? I can't tell that either. Already I've lost the distance you need in order to judge someone.

Because when she sees me she smiles crookedly, one side of her mouth quirking up a little, the way (is this memory or merely longing?) my mother once smiled.

I ask if she needs help, and she says, please. I hold the front door open so she can push the armchair out to the curb, only I miscalculate and let go too soon, and the door catches her wrist.

"It's okay, no, really," she says, over my apologies. "It doesn't hurt."

Later I'll see the bruise, swelled purple over the wrist-bone. Even later, I'll think of omens.

She takes me up to her apartment and makes me chai, boiled thick and red-brown and fragrant with cloves. To welcome me, she says. Pouring, she turns her wrist, and there it is, delicate and deadly as a bracelet sewn into her skin, the scar.

"My name is Radhika," says Malik's second wife, handing me a thin, gold-edged cup.

"Mine is Mira."

Over soft tea steam we smile at our shared, ironic legacy, both of us named after women of myth, women whose lives men had tried to ruin.

———

THIS FRIDAY AFTERNOON I sit on a chair in Radhika's kitchen and feel the sun seep into my bones like the jabakusum oil she is rubbing into my hair. The room is filled with a sweet, sleepy smell out of my childhood. Her fingers make little circles on my scalp. They trace the small dip behind each earlobe.

I moved in here a week ago. Priya had gone back to India to get married, and a new family needed her apartment. Radhika had been asked to find me a room with someone else, but instead she said, "Why don't you stay with me? I have more space than I need." It had felt so right that I hadn't even needed to ask if she were sure.

"Next page," she says.

I'm holding a book in my lap, a big library book with a blue-and-gold cover titled *The Great Deserts of the American West*. I read, "The blooming season for cacti is very short, a few weeks at most in the spring. But during this time the barren and sere landscape is transformed by the vibrant coronets of hedgehog cactus, candy cactus and prickly pear that push out through the plants' spiny armament."

We do this a lot, look at books together. Radhika is hesitant in English, so usually I am the reader. But she is the interpreter of details I would have passed over.

"Look," she says, pointing at a picture, and I see how, after their brief flowering, only thorns are left on the plants. I don't know much about cacti; I have always imagined their thorns to be stinging, poisonous. But in this photograph the evening light has caught their fineness so that they shine, exalted, like the hair of infants.

I want to say something to Radhika about the unexpected, redemptive beauty of the world, but the phone rings.

"Yes?" she says.

I can hear the voice inside the receiver, tinnily obsequious. "Malik-ji will be sending the car eight P.M. sharp this evening, as usual, madam. Please to be ready downstairs."

Radhika's fingers tighten on the receiver. But no. I am mistaken. Her tone is as calm as always when she says, "Tell him sorry, I'm not well today." When the voice, sounding unhappy, protests that Malik-ji will be bahut-bahut upset, she repeats the sentence patiently, as though to a child. Then she hangs up.

The silence bristles between us like a live wire. In the months we've known each other, she has talked of many things—but not Malik, or the Fridays when his limousine glides up silent as some submarine creature to the curb and opens its hinged jaw.

I know what I should ask now. *Why did you?* A question which ebbs like a wave back to that day at a village wedding when she grew aware of a man's desirous eyes. A question which gathers itself to sweep forward to the hour when she opened a tap, mixed the warm and cold right, so it wouldn't hurt, held the wrist just so under the gush of it. *Why did you?* A question that breaks over this moment now, the cool danger of her voice saying *no,* what it might mean.

But I'm afraid to ask. I've lost so much already. Besides, what would I say if someone knew to ask *me* why? As in *Why didn't you insist that your mother remain with you that day on the terrace?*

Radhika's fingers are back in my hair, their circling unhurried, as though there had been no interruption. She nudges me with her hip. "Go on," she says, saving me, and thankfully I turn the page.

AJIT IS A regular at our restaurant. He used to come once in a while, but recently it's every week, sometimes two or even three times. Which surprises me, because he's not the kind of Indian man the place attracts. Our men are usually middle-aged, balding, a little down at the heel. H-1 visa holders whose shoulders slump under the hopes of wives and children waiting back in the home country. Who want a down-home meal that doesn't cost too much and like to order the specials. (The younger Indians, the ones who want to impress their American girlfriends, go to Khyber Palace down the street, where they have Indian karaoke and disco bhangra on Saturday nights.) Ajit's shoes are laced and eagerly polished, his shirts are the button-down kind with all the buttons firmly sewed on. And though he doesn't have on a jacket or a tie, I get the feeling he's just taken them off and placed them, carefully folded, on the passenger seat of his car. There's a certain trustfulness about him that makes it clear he has never lived anywhere except America.

What I like about Ajit is the way he seems to be at home in a room full of people who are nothing like him. Perhaps he isn't aware of how different he is from us? He jokes with the waiters—he's wildly popular with them, and not just for the substantial tips he leaves behind—watches the other customers with unabashed curiosity, eats with gusto. Even Malik, the one time he dropped by, patted his shoulder and said, "Ah, Ajit, just the person I wanted to see!" He brought him up to the register and introduced us. "This is our Mira, a college graduate, just like you. Sharp as a needle. Hang around her and you'll learn everything you want to know about India."

I gave him a sharp-as-a-needle glance. Was he being sarcastic? If he was, it escaped Ajit. Or perhaps he was the kind of person sarcasm couldn't touch. He shook my hand with a wide-open smile and said, "Delighted," like he meant it.

Since then Ajit has taken to stopping at the register to chat before he leaves. I am a little astonished at his frankness. Are all second-generation Indians like this? Already I know that he's in finance, that he's been out here for two years working for a small start-up company. His mother is a schoolteacher and his father an engineer back in the little midwestern town where he grew up. He gets lonely for them sometimes, but thinks California is wildly exciting, mostly because of all the different kinds of South Asians he has been meeting. He doesn't have a girlfriend yet, but is hopeful. When he leaves with a cheery "Take care!" I stare after him in envy.

IN HIS LETTERS my brother asks if I like it here, if people are kind to me. My sister-in-law adds, Is the weather better than Texas? Have you been down to San Francisco yet? Now that you've settled down, what are your future plans?

I consider replying that I've found someone with whom to read books, who is more than kind. I think of different words to describe Radhika: friend, sister, mother. (But none of them are right.) The weather is humid and exasperatingly un-Californian. (But to admit this would be a defeat.) As for San Francisco and my future, I have left them both alone. I am happy with what I have: a brief reprieve in which I can float without thought, as in a warm bath. (Then I'm ashamed: I should have been more industrious and taken a day-trip on the Golden State Bus Line; I should have enrolled for a course at the University of California Extension.)

And so I don't write back.

THAT DAY, AFTER the phone call from Malik's henchman, Radhika and I looked at one last photograph in the desert book. It was the picture of a woman holding out a handful of sand. WOMAN MINER PANS FOR GOLD, INYO COUNTY, read the caption. The woman wore jeans with frayed knees, a vest of some sort, a broad-brimmed hat which pulled her face into its oval of darkness. She didn't look at the camera but at something (someone?) whose shadow fell across the edge of the photograph—coyote perhaps, or a horse. Her lips were parted in a small, secret smile.

ON FRIDAY EVENING, Ajit taps his fingers on the register, slides a card shyly at me, and clears his throat to ask if

I'd go out with him. Next Friday, maybe? My head is full of a dim vibration. I open my mouth to say no. But when I look, he has the eyes of an antelope. And here's another surprise: the way my heart thuds inside my chest, like runner's feet, light and rapid, *why not, why not.*

Perhaps this, at last, will be how I climb out of my water tank.

When I go to the back office to ask the manager if I can have next Friday night off, he throws up his hands. "Absolutely not possible," he says. "We don't have anyone to take your place."

"How about Ramesh? I could do his lunchtime shift, and he—"

"You must be joking. That banana-fingered bumbler? Every day after lunch we are spending one hour correcting all the things he rung up wrong."

"Come on," I say. I've gained a certain weight around here since I started sharing Radhika's apartment, and I attempt to use it. "It's just for one day!"

"What so-important thing is happening next Friday?"

I tell him about Ajit, and he throws up his hands again. "Dating with a boy who's no better than an Amreekan! Nothing except trouble in it! Chee chee, what would your mother say!"

A hardness twists its way along my shoulder bones.

"That's none of your business," I say through rigid lips.

Then I hear the soft voice at the door: "What's all this hallah about?"

It's Malik, who seems to have a knack for appearing magically. Perhaps that is the key to his success? He is dressed with more care than usual, in a beautiful dark suit— the way I'd originally imagined him. With his glossy new haircut, he is almost dashing. His tie looks like silk, looks like he's on his way to someplace important, a party perhaps in some glittery penthouse, uniformed servers carrying silver trays.

Then a thought comes to me. It's Friday—could it be for Radhika that he has dressed?

When the manager has poured out his complaints, he says, "A date, hanh? Our Mira wants to go on a date?" His eyes move over me, appraising but absent, as though he is thinking of something else. In the corridor's shadows, his expression is hooded, satyrlike. Finally he says, "Perhaps *that's* what she needs."

My cheeks burn. What does he mean?

But already he's turned a suave smile on the manager. "Oh, don't be such an old fogey. Let the girl go. And give her an advance so she can get something fancy to wear."

Still smiling, he stands back courteously to let me pass. The cologne he is wearing—understated as only the most expensive ones are—follows me down the dark corridor like a suspicion I can't quite put into words.

THE EVENING LIGHT is rich and gold this Friday, the day of my date with Ajit, and when I enter our apartment, the tiny mirrors on the sofa cushions Radhika finished embroidering last week dance and wink. The room is filled with a smell I know well—there they are, a platter of samosas, sitting on the kitchen counter, ready for frying.

"Is that you, Mira?" Radhika calls from her room. "Good timing! I just finished filling the samosas. Let me fry you a couple."

I set down the packages I'm carrying and collapse on the sofa. My feet hurt, and my head. Already I'm regretting my extravagance, wondering if what I've bought is all wrong.

I've never been a good shopper. Even in India, where you sit on a large white sheet spread under a cool ceiling fan and drink Jusla and point while the storekeeper takes out one sari after another and tells you the name of each and where it came from, I would ask my mother to do my shopping. She always knew what was suitable for a particular occasion, what would look good on me.

Radhika comes out of her room wearing a thin batik robe that molds itself to her body as she walks. She moves, like many Indian women, with delicate, careful steps which hardly disturb the air around her. Her hips ripple under the silky robe. It's a new one, and beautiful, but not something you would go out in. My heart beats out of rhythm. Did she refuse Malik again?

"I bet you're wondering how I knew you weren't working this evening!" From the kitchen Radhika throws me a mischievous smile. "One of the girls downstairs mentioned that Ramesh would be doing his first evening shift—the entire restaurant is nervous about it! So I thought this would be the perfect time to make you some samosas—I know how much you like them—and chat a little." The oil sputters as she turns the stuffed triangles that must have taken her hours to prepare. "There's something I've been wanting to tell you."

She brings me a plate of golden-crisp samosas and a bowl of deep brown tamarind chutney, and sits across from me. Her face is flushed and lovely. I give the clock a hasty, guilty glance. In a few minutes I'm going to have to tell her about my evening plans.

"When I met Malik," Radhika says, "I was so young, just a village girl. I thought being the wife of a rich man was the best thing that could happen to a woman." Her lashes tremble darkly against her cheek as she looks down. "When he told the matchmaker he was mad for me, that he'd do anything to marry me, I couldn't believe it. I was so proud to be desired by such a successful man, I didn't stop to think of anything else. My parents didn't want to send me so far away, with a man they knew so little about, but I persuaded them. I insisted I'd be happy with him. And then I got to America and found out about his—" Her voice splinters apart.

"Radhika—" I reach for her hand—"maybe it's better if you don't talk about such—"

"No." She is crying, openly, unashamedly. Her hand closes on mine the way, in the Bombay ocean, a woman's might have closed upon sea froth at the last minute—as though it could hold her up. "I've had enough of silences. But it's not Malik I want to talk about. I learned to live with him years ago—like I learned to live with this." She turns her wrist to gaze at her scar. Then she looks at me, her lashes spiky with tears. "No. It's something quite different I want to tell you. Something sudden, like a summer rainstorm. Something that's given me more happiness than I hoped to have in this life."

I hate myself for what I'm going to say next. But it isn't merely selfishness that drives me, it is also a fear I cannot articulate.

"I'm terribly sorry, Radhika. Can we talk about this later tonight? I have to go out. I promised"—I stumble over the next word—"a friend."

She lets go of my hand right away. Wipes her eyes. "Then of course you must." Her voice is polite, but I hear the hurt in it.

"We'll talk as soon as I come back—it's just a couple of hours. . . ."

"Yes," she says distantly, then goes into her room. When, dressed in my new clothes, I knock to say that I'm leaving, she doesn't answer. I stand in front of the shut bedroom door, guilty as a teenager. I know I should turn the knob, go inside. But I don't. Right now I need to feel confident. And I know Radhika would disapprove of the lacy white dress which stops at my thighs, the stiletto heels in which I stumble a little, the glittery crimson out-lining my mouth. My flyaway hair from which I've sham-pooed all traces of the jabakusum oil she rubbed in with such care.

WHEN AJIT SEES me, he lets out a long whistle. "I'd planned a quiet dinner." He laughs. "But now I see we've got to go dancing."

So that's what we do. And even though I've never danced in my life, in the dimly lit nightclub where music ricochets off every glistening surface, and swaying bodies brush against us unselfconsciously, I find that I can do it. I shimmy my shoulders and throw back my head, dancing my way into the new life I'd begun to dream—it seems so long ago—on the Greyhound bus. When Ajit spins me so I end up against his chest, I don't shove away as an earlier Mira would have done, the Mira on whose hair rust flecks from a water tank had settled like dried blood. I lean there a moment, savoring the wholesome, lemony smell of his skin. When after a walk along the riverfront with its glimmering waters, he kisses me, I find it pleasant, and not the disgusting, spit-and-groping occurrence I'd feared. And when, somewhat timidly, he asks if I would come to his apartment, I am not outraged or even embarrassed. I lay my fingers lightly on his lips, as a woman in a movie might do, a dangerous woman, and say, with a smile, "Not yet."

IT'S AFTER MIDNIGHT when I open the door of our apartment. Inside, all is silent. Dark. I slip off my heels, tiptoe toward my room.

"Mira, do you know how late it is! I was so worried!" Radhika's voice is a whip, lashing out of blackness. When she flicks on the light, it blinds me.

She's still wearing the batik robe. It's wrinkled now, and her hair, come undone, is mussed as though she's been running her hands through it.

"I'm sorry—"

Now she notices my dress, the high heels I'm holding. "Where did you go?" she asks hoarsely. "With whom?"

My cheeks are hot, but I lift my chin. "I went dancing—with my friend Ajit."

"Dancing! With your *friend* Ajit!" Her voice is thick. She takes a step toward me. "Look at you—out all night with some man, half-naked in that dress—" Her eyes take in my hair, my makeup, stop on my mouth, kissed bare of lipstick and a little swollen. "Like . . . like a common—"

"Like what?" I'm angry too, now. What gives her the right to talk to me this way? "Like you?"

Her eyes widen in shock. For a moment she's silent. Then she says, very quietly, "Not like me, Mira. I'd never want you to be like me. To make my mistakes. To end up tied to the man who tricked you in the worst way, because what else is possible in your life—"

There's something heavy in her voice, about to break open. To forestall it, I shout, "Stop trying to be my mother."

"Your mother!" Radhika makes a small sound in her

throat that could be a laugh. "I don't want to be your mother. I only want to save you from the suffering I see you rushing toward." She puts her hands on my shoulders. "If I could take all the pain from your life into mine, I'd do it right now. Mira, my dear." She pushes away a wisp of hair from my face, kisses my cheek. "My love," she says. Then her lips are on mine.

For a moment or a lifetime, I stand stunned, surprised and yet not so, trying to make sense of what's happening. Trying to make sense of my body, the shivering that rises up from the soles of my feet. Do my lips want to kiss her back? Do my treacherous arms want to crush her softness against mine? Then I thrust her away.

"No," I whisper. "No." My voice shakes with horror. But who am I horrified by? My shoes have clattered to the floor. As I stumble to the apartment door, I hear Radhika cry, "Mira, don't go—" Then I slam it shut.

I STAND ON the curb outside our building, shivering. When numbness has seeped into all the bones of my bare feet, I call Ajit from the pay phone. I am not sure what I will do if Radhika comes looking for me. When she doesn't, I'm not sure if it's thankfulness I feel.

The choices in our lives, what impels us to them?

A few late-night folks pass by. I cringe back against the wall, but they don't seem to notice me. Perhaps an Indian girl, barefoot in a gauzy white mini, is a common sight to them. Perhaps they have worse problems of their own.

Ajit's car takes the corner too sharply, screeches to a stop.

"Mira, what happened?"

Dressed in sweats and sleep-tousled, he seems startled and young. Too young, I think tiredly.

"God, you're freezing," he says as he shepherds me into the car. He pulls off his windbreaker and guides my arms through its sleeves. In his apartment, while I sit on the couch and stare at the wall, he brings me a pair of woolen socks. When I begin to cry, he puts an awkward arm around me, not sure of what to do.

Inside I am split in two. One Mira watches the other crying, tries to figure out why. Is it Ajit's kindness? Or the loss of the only friendship in my life? Are they for a mother who believed she must keep her daughter safe at any cost, these belated tears? Or for myself, being sucked into a vortex from which whispered words rise like ancestral ghosts: *disgusting, perverted, unnatural.*

I turn to Ajit, pull his face to mine, press my lips on his. When he says he doesn't think it's a good idea, I'm too upset right now, I hold him tighter. I will the pounding in my head to grow louder, to drown my thoughts. I rake my nails across Ajit's back and hear him gasp. I tug off his sweatshirt and kiss whatever I come across—earlobe, throat, the curved line of his collarbone. He no longer protests. Against my mouth, his skin is salt and smoke. My head is exploding. Briefly, before the pounding pulls me under, I wonder if a woman's skin would have tasted different.

THERE IS, IN empty apartments, a certain shifting of energy, an absence of breathed air. I feel this as soon as I open the door to Radhika's place. But I am too exhausted to wonder where she is at 3:00 A.M. Or where I will go when I leave this place, as I know I must.

I stumble to the bathroom and start the water. I kick off the too-large men's sandals that Ajit had insisted on giving me, shrug off his jacket. I'll leave them for him at the restaurant. My own clothes—the lace dress ripped carelessly under the arm, the panties stained with blood, I throw into the wastebasket. My aim is shaky. The basket tips over, spilling crumpled wads of paper over the bathroom floor.

Sex had been a disappointment. I hadn't expected pleasure, but I had hoped for ecstasy—in the way the Greeks had meant the word. Something that took you out of your-self, made you forget who you were.

In Ajit's bed, no matter what I attempted, I remained myself, caught in my unresponsive flesh like the seed inside a hard, green mango. When finally he took my face in his hands and said, trying to mask his disappointment, "It's okay, Mira, stop now. We'll try again another day," I closed my eyes, shamed by his generosity. I knew there wouldn't be another day.

The water sends a welcome shock of heat through me as I climb in. I should be soaping myself clean, but I'm too tired. I lie there and watch the ripples of reflected light on white porcelain, on wet brown skin. In the stillness, it is easy to drift into other waters. Orange peels floating down, humid air that clogs the throat. When the knocking be-gins, I have to put a hand over my mouth to stifle my scream.

But it is only one of the downstairs girls. "Sorry to dis-turb you so early," she says. "But I heard the water run-ning, so I knew you were up. Do you know Radhika's in the hospital?" She nods to confirm the question in my eyes. "Yes, another suicide attempt. Late last night, in Malik-ji's apartment. She took his sleeping pills this time. Luckily they found her before it was too late. Listen, you better sit down, you don't look so good. . . ."

THE WAITING ROOM of the hospital is unbearably cheery with pastel printed sofas and posters of baby animals peering from behind unlikely objects. I sit on a bench out in the corridor, taking comfort in its plain hardness, in the way my back begins to ache after a while. Sooner or later they must allow visitors to see Radhika.

"Are you family?" the nurse had asked. I tried to say yes. But I'm only good at lying to myself.

"Sorry," said the nurse.

Radhika must have called Malik late that night, saying she felt better. She asked him to send the limo, to meet her at his apartment, as they always did. After it was over and he left for his other home—his real home, the mansion up on the hills where his wife and sons slept—she must have done it then. She reached under the bathroom sink where he kept the pills, and smiled a bitter smile. She knew all his secrets now. She looked out the window at his Porsche, its ruby lights receding into fog—but she was the one who was leaving, who was gone already. Out of my life, taking the honorable way, enduring this final night with Malik so I wouldn't have to be the one to find her body. She had planned it all— except that when she said to the limo driver, "Take me back to my apartment tomorrow, I'm too tired right now," he had called Malik to check if that was all right.

———

AFTER THE GIRL from downstairs had left, I went back into the bathroom. I let the water out of the tub and watched its downward spinning, at once lazy and urgent. I wiped my wet footprints and righted the wastebasket, picking the wadded sheets off the floor. On an impulse I smoothed them out.

There were three of them. One said, *Mira* . . . One said, *I never expected* . . . The last was a poem of sorts.

> *In the desert of my heart,*
> *you, cactus flower,*
> *blooming without thorn.*

When she wrote those words, I was dancing. I twirled on tiptoe, making myself tall. My hair wild with abandonment, I let Ajit pull me into his chest, into the possibilities of my new American life.

I THINK NOTHING of the footsteps, muffled on hospital carpeting, until they stop in front of me. Then I look up and it is Malik. His eyes are swollen and I see, with wonder, that he's been weeping. When he speaks to me, the words glow with hate.

"We were happy until you got here, until you put your

sick ideas into her head. I should have gotten rid of you right at the first, when she started acting different. But I didn't—wouldn't—believe that she could..." A spasm shakes him and he looks away. When he turns back, his voice is cool and serrated. "I'm giving you twenty-four hours to leave."

I watch him as he walks down the hallway, his right leg dragging a little in a limp I had never noticed. It comes to me that the stories about him are true. But I am too full of other emotions to feel fear. How ironic that of the three of us, he was the one to first smell the change in the air. He brought Ajit over to the cash register, he made the manager give me the evening off for my date. *Maybe that's what she needs.* I had thought, naively, that he was talking about me. But he was talking about the woman he loved in spite of himself, the one person who had shown him how, while you tighten your fist around a life, the heart can slip away.

IT TAKES ME only an hour to pack my belongings. I should leave for the bank now, get out what little money I have. Then the Greyhound station, where I need to check the schedule, decide on my destination. Instead I wander through the apartment, touching a table mat Radhika painted, the roses—now dying—that she arranged in a brass vase. I think how I've turned out to be all that I dreamed of on the bus—burning wind, bramble bush, things that scorch and scrape. But none of them is what I imagined. It had not struck me that a lit fuse must burn itself first, before setting the world on fire.

Finally, because I must, I go into Radhika's bedroom.

Radhika's room reflects her neatness. The bedspread is creaseless, the photos of her parents hang straight and level with each other. Even last night, after getting ready, when there was no longer any need, she had put everything back in its place. Face powder, deodorant, perfume, hair oil. They stand lined up on her dresser, precise, giving nothing away. Comb, brush, filigreed hand mirror. Kumkum powder in a silver box. I pick each one up, try to think what she had thought. Then I see the book.

Splayed at the far end of the dresser, it is the only thing that is out of place. *The Great Deserts of the American West,* turned to the picture where the miner squinches her eyes against the glare of sun on sand.

I carry the book to Radhika's bed. When I lay my head on her pillow, it seems I smell her hair.

Down at the Greyhound station, the drivers are starting the engines, lifting their feet off the brakes. The buses begin to roll down the highway, each taking you to a different destiny.

Did the woman in the photo take a bus the day she moved to the hills? How many people had spoken to her in my sister-in-law's voice, saying what she was doing, it just wasn't right, wasn't natural?

She would have shrugged her shoulders, turned her face a little. Maybe she smiled that small, secret smile.

Who is to say? If a woman finds joy in the spare, pared flesh of the desert, if she finds joy in another woman's sand-brown body, who is to say?

There are so many words I'm searching for, I who had stopped believing in their possibility. In the hospital, as I slip past the nurse's station, as I look in each room for Radhika, I hope some of them will come to me. She will turn her head away; her earring will glint like an evaporation of dew. But this time around, I've learned insistence. On the long bus ride south, and later, in sand and rock, among the fierce momentary blooming of cacti, I'll lean my head into her shoulder. I'll run my fingers over her scar the way one reads Braille. Perhaps I'll find them there, the words for my night with Ajit. The water tank. The women swimming out into the Bombay ocean. For my mother, who also believed that to save the one you love, you have to give up your own life.

On the way out, I glance at the book, the miner holding out her cupped palm, daring us to decipher what in it is sand, and what gold. I decide I know whom she is smiling at. It is her lover, the woman whose shadow has entered the photograph, and in doing so shifted the balance of light.

THE UNKNOWN ERRORS
OF OUR LIVES

RUCHIRA IS PACKING when she discovers the notebook in a dusty alcove of her apartment. It is sandwiched between a high school group photo in which she smiles tensely at the camera, her hair hacked short around her ears in a style that was popular that year, and a box of brittle letters, the sheets tinged with blue and smelling faintly of sweet betel nut, from her grandmother, who is now dead. For a moment she fingers the book's limp purple cover, its squished spiral binding, and wonders what's inside, it's been that long since she wrote in it. Then she remembers. Of course! It's her book of errors, from her midteens, a time she thinks back on now as her Earnest Period.

She imagines telling Biren about it. "I was a gawky girl with a mouth full of braces and a head full of ideas for self-improvement."

"And then?" he would ask.

"Then I turned twenty-six, and decided I was perfect just the way I was."

In response, Biren would laugh his silent laugh, which began at the upturned outer edges of his eyes and rippled through him like wind on water. He was the only person she knew who laughed like that, soundlessly, offering his whole body to the act. It made her heart feel like a popcorn popper where all the kernels have burst into neon yellow. She'd respond with a small smile, the kind she hoped made her appear alluring and secretive, but inside she'd be weak with gratitude that he found her so funny.

That, and the way he looked at her paintings. Because otherwise she doesn't think she could have agreed to marry him.

TO THINK THAT none of this would have happened, that she wouldn't be sitting here this beautiful rainy morning, pale blue like jacarandas, packing, getting ready to move out of her Berkeley apartment into their newlywed condo in San Francisco in two weeks, if she hadn't mumbled an ungracious agreement when her mother said, "Why don't you meet him, Ru? Kamala Mashi writes so highly of him. Meet him once and see how you like each other." Ruchira shudders when she realizes how close she had come to saying No, she wasn't interested, she'd rather use the time to go to Lashay's and get her hair done. Just because Aunt Kamala had written, *Not only is the boy just two years older than our Ruchira and handsome looking, 173 centimeters tall, and holds a fast-rising job in the renowned Charles Schwab financial company, he is also a nephew of the Boses of Tullygunge—you recall them, a fine, upright family—and to top it all he has intelligently decided to follow our time-tested traditions in his search for a bride.* It would have been the worst error of her life, and she wouldn't even have known it. It saddens her to think of all the errors people make (she has been musing over such things lately)—the unknown errors of their lives, the ones they can never put down in a book and are therefore doomed to repeat.

But she had shown up at the Café Trieste, sullen in old blue jeans and a severe ponytail that yanked her eyebrows into a skeptic arch, and met Biren, and been charmed.

"It's because you were so wary, even more than me," she told him later. "You'd been reading—wasn't it one of those depressingly high-minded Russians?"

"Dostoyevsky. Brought along for the precise purpose of impressing you."

"And for the first fifteen minutes of our conversation, you kept your finger in the book, marking your place, as though you couldn't wait to get back to it."

"You mean it wasn't my suave Johnny Depp looks that got you? I'm disappointed."

"Dream on," she said, and gave him a little push. Actually, she'd been rather taken by the stud he wore in his ear. Its small, beckoning glint in the smoke-fogged café had made him seem foreign and dangerous, set him apart from the Indian men she knew, at least the ones who would have agreed to meet a daughter-of-a-friend-of-a-distant-relative for late-afternoon coffee with matrimony in mind. But most of all she liked that he admitted up front to feeling sheepish, sitting like this in a café after having declared, for all those arrogant years (just as she had), that *he'd* never have anything to do with an arranged marriage.

"But the alternative—it doesn't seem to work that well, does it?" he would say later, shrugging, and she'd agree, thinking back on all the boys she had dated in college, Indian boys and white boys and black boys and even, once, a young man from Bolivia with green eyes. At a certain point they had all wanted something from her, she didn't know what it was exactly, only that she hadn't been willing—or able—to give it. It wasn't just the sex, though that too she'd shied away from. What throwback gene was it that stopped her, a girl born in America? What cautionary spore released by her grandmother over her cradle when Ruchira's parents took her to India? Sooner or later, the boyfriends fell away. She saw them as though through the wrong end of a telescope, their faces urgent or surly, mouthing words she could no longer hear.

THUMBING THROUGH HER book of errors, Ruchira thinks this must be one of life's most Machiavellian revenges: one day you look back at your teenage self and realize exactly how excruciatingly clueless you were, more so even than you had thought your parents to be. And pompous to boot. Here, for example, is the quotation she'd copied out in her tight, painstaking handwriting: *An unexamined life is not worth living.* As if a fourteen-year-old had any idea of what an examined life was. The notion of tracking errors possesses some merit, except that *her* errors were so puerile, so everygirl. The time she told Marta that she thought Kevin was cute, only to have that information relayed back to her, with crude anatomical elaborations, from the walls of the girls' bathroom. The time she drank too many rum-and-cokes at Susie's party and threw up on the living room carpet. The time she believed Dr. Vikram, who wore maroon suspenders and gave her a summer job in his dental office, to be so cool—and then he made a groping pass at her.

She tosses the purple notebook onto the growing pile of things to be recycled. (Recycling mistakes, now that's a thought!) She's come to terms with misjudgments and slippages, she's resigned to the fact that they'll always be a part of her life. If there are errorless people in the world, she doesn't want to know them. She's certain they'll be eminently disagreeable. That's something else she likes about Biren—all the mistakes he has already admitted to. How he dropped out of college for a semester during his freshman year to play electric guitar with a band aptly named The Disasters. How late one night, coming back to the city from Sausalito, he gave a ride to a hitchhiker of indeterminate sex only to have him/her try to throw him/herself from the car and off the Golden Gate bridge. How, for a short time last year, he got involved with a woman who had a knife tattooed on her chest, even though he knew she did drugs.

Ruchira was shocked and enthralled. She wasn't sure why he was telling her all this. To impress her? To start clean? To gain her (or was it his own) forgiveness? Small disquiets nipped at the edge of her mind like minnows; she let them slip away. Questions filled her mouth. What had he lost by jilting Tina Turner for Standard and Poor? What had he said to the hitchhiker to stop her—Ruchira was sure it was a woman—from jumping? (He *had* tried to stop her, hadn't he?) What made him break up, finally, with the knife-woman?

She pushed the questions into a corner of her cheek like hard candy, saving them for later. Meanwhile, he was the most exciting man she knew. His was a geography of suicide bridges and tattoo parlors, night concert alleys and skyscrapers rising into the sky like blocks of black ice. A galaxy far, far away from the blandness of auto-malls and AMC cinemas which she'd never really escaped, not even by moving from her parents' suburban house to Berkeley. But now conjugality would confer that same excitement on her.

HE SAW THE paintings when he came to pick her up for a concert. They'd discovered a common interest in classical Indian music, and Chaurasia was playing at the Zellerbach. She had not intended for him to come up to the apartment—she felt she didn't know him well enough. She was going to meet him downstairs when he rang the buzzer. But one of the other tenants must have let him in because here he was, knocking on her door. For a panicked moment she thought of not opening it, pretending she wasn't there, calling him later with a fabricated disaster.

He was severely suave in a jacket with a European cut and, although the sun had set already, dark glasses in which she could see herself, convex and bulbous-headed. She felt mortified. Behind her, she knew, paint rags were strewn across the floor. A cereal bowl left by the armchair, swollen flecks of bran drowning in bluish milk. A half-eaten packet of Cheetos on the counter. Jelly jars of turpentine with brushes soaking in them on the coffee table. The canvas she'd been working on (and which was totally wrong, she knew it already) was the only thing she'd managed to put away.

"Very nice," he said, lightly touching the sleeve of her short black cocktail dress. But already he was looking beyond her at the canvases hanging on the wall.

"You didn't tell me you paint," he said accusingly.

This was true. She had told him a lot of things about herself, but they were all carefully chosen to be shielding and secondary. Her work as events coordinator in an art gallery, which she liked because the people she met had such intense opinions, mostly about other people's art. Her favorite college class, "Myth and Literature" in junior year, which she had picked quite by chance because

"Interpersonal Communication" was full. The trip she took two winters back to New Zealand to stay for a few nights in a Maori village—only to discover that it had water beds in the more expensive rooms and a Jacuzzi strategically positioned among the lava rocks. She felt bad now about her duplicity, her reluctance to give of herself, that old spiral with her boyfriends starting again.

He'd moved close to the wall and was standing very still. It took her a moment to figure out that he was examining her brushstrokes. (But only artists did that. Was he a closet artist, too?) Finally he moved back and let out a long, incredulous breath, and it struck her that she had been holding hers as well. "Tell me about your work," he said.

This was hard. She had started painting two years ago, and had never talked to anyone about it. Even her parents didn't know. When they came for dinner, she removed the canvases from the wall and hid them in her closet. She sprayed the room with Eucalyptus Mist and lit incense sticks so they wouldn't smell the turpentine. The act of painting was the first really risky thing she had done in her life. Being at the gallery, she knew how different her work was from everything in there, or in the glossy art journals. Her technique was crude—she hadn't taken classes and didn't intend to. She would probably never amount to much. Still, she came back from work every evening and painted furiously. She worked late into the night, light-headed with the effort to remember. She stopped inviting people over. She made excuses when her friends wanted her to go out. She had to force herself to return their calls, and often she didn't. She ruined canvas after canvas, slashed them in frustration and threw them into the Dumpster behind the building. She wept till she saw a blurry brightness, like sunspots, wherever she looked. Then, miraculously, she got better. Sometimes now, at 2.00 A.M., or 3:00, her back muscles tight and burning, a stillness would rise around her, warm and vaporous. Held within it, she would hear, word for word, the stories her grandmother used to tell.

Ruchira has seen her grandmother no more than a dozen times in her life, once every two or three years during summer vacation, when her parents visited India. She loves her more than she loves anyone else, more than her parents. She knows this to be unfair; they are good parents and have always done the best they can for her in their earnest, Quaker Oatmeal way. She had struggled through the Bengali alphabet, submitting to years of classes at that horrible weekend school run by bulge-eyed Mrs. Duttagupta, just so she would be able to read her grandmother's letters and reply to them without asking her parents to intervene. When a letter arrived from India, she slept with it for nights, a faint crackling under her pillow. When she had trouble making up her mind about something, she asked herself, What would Thakuma do? Ah, the flawed logic of loving! Surprisingly, it helped her, although she was continents and generations apart, in a world whose values must have been unimaginable to a woman who had been married at sixteen and widowed at twenty-four, and who had only left Calcutta once in her entire life for a pilgrimage to Badrinath with the members of her Geeta group.

Someday she plans to tell Biren all this.

When her grandmother died two summers back of a heart attack, Ruchira spent an entire week in bed. She refused to go to India for the funeral, though maybe she should have, because she dreamed over and over what she had thought she couldn't bear to look at. The hard orange thrust of the flames of the cremation pyre, the hair going first, in a short, manic burst of light, the skin warping like wood, the eyeballs melting, her grandmother's face blackening and collapsing in on itself with terrible finality. It didn't help that her parents told her that the event, which occurred in a modern crematorium rather than the traditional burning ghats, was quick and sanitary and invisible.

She started the paintings soon after that.

"It's a series." Ruchira stammered now, speaking too fast. "Mythic images from Indian legends. I've only managed to complete three so far. The first is Hanuman, the monkey god, carrying the magic herb that can bring you back to life—you know the story? When Lakshman was hurt in battle, and Hanuman plucked up an entire mountain because he wasn't sure which herb he was supposed to bring back . . . ?" She'd painted Hanuman in purples and blues and looped his tail in an elegant, gentlemanly manner over an arm. In his right hand he held a miniature mountain the way one might hold a box of chocolates when paying a visit. She had given him a human face, her father's (unexpectedly, she'd turned out to be good at portraits), his expression of puzzled kindness. She remembered the ecstatic day when the idea had first swooped down on her like a taloned angel. Now the painting looked fanciful, garish. It made her blush.

"But it's brilliant. They're all brilliant," Biren said. "An amazing concept. I've never seen anything like it. This next one, isn't that the magic cow, what's her name, who possesses all the riches of the world—"

"Kama dhenu," she supplied shyly, delighted by his recognition. The cow in the painting reclined on a cloud, her chin resting on demure, folded forelegs. A shower of gold coins fanned out from her hooves, carpeting the earth below. Her white wings were as tidily pleated as a widow's sari. Around her head, words from old stories arched in a rainbow. *Long long ago. Beyond the fields of Tepantar. Once there was a poor brahmin who had a clever wife. And the snake carried a jewel on its head.* Her stubborn, alert face was that of Ruchira's grandmother.

By the time they got to the third painting, it was too late to go to the concert and Ruchira no longer stammered. With precise gestures she explained to Biren that the huge eagle creature was Jatayu, who died trying to save Sita from the evil ten-headed Ravana as he was abducting her. In Ruchira's painting Jatayu's feathers were saffron and white and green, the colors of the Indian flag. His face was that of her grandfather, whom she only knew from sepia photographs because he died long before she was born—in the Andaman prisons, where the British used to send freedom fighters. Her grandmother had told her the story. They had caught him making bombs, he'd been part of a conspiracy to assassinate Lord Minto, the hated governorgeneral. In Ruchira's painting, Ravana, pasty-faced and with a prominent overbite, was clearly British, and Jatayu had knocked off all his bowler hats with one giant swipe of his claw.

"I love it!" said Biren. "I just love it!"

They kissed their first kiss soon after that. He tasted of

salted sunflower seeds (his secret weakness, she would learn later). His tongue was thin and pointy and intelligent. She doesn't remember leading him to the bedroom, only that they were there already, lying on the crumpled blue bed-cover, his fingers, her fingers, the small hollow inside his elbow and the vein pulsing in it. She thought she could see a faint radiation of heat where their skins touched. Did his hair smell of lemons? In her hurry she tore a loose button off his shirt. (Later they would laugh about that.) The back of his ear stud rasped her hand, raising a weal. He brought it to his mouth and licked it. The small mirrors embroidered into the bedcover pressed their cool disks against her bare back, then against his. His nipples were brown and hard as apple seeds in her mouth.

Then his hands were on hers, tight, stopping her as she tugged on his zipper.

"Don't. It isn't safe. I didn't expect this. I don't have anything with me. And I take it you don't either. . . ."

The blood rocked so hard in the hollows of her body, she feared she'd break open. He had to repeat himself before she could understand the words. She shook her head vaguely, not caring. She wouldn't let go. Her body, thwarted so long, had seized on wildness like a birthright. A part of her cried, *You're insane, girl.* She pushed her face against him, his chest hairs wiry against her tongue, until finally his hands were gone. She could feel fingers, their drowning grip on her hair. She heard him say something. The words were too close, out of focus. Later she would think they had started with *God*. As in *God I hope you know what you're doing*.

JUST THREE DAYS left before her wedding, and Ruchira thinks, Does anyone ever know what they're really doing? What the tightening of certain muscles and the letting go of others, the aspiration of certain vowels and the holding back of others, will lead to? What terrifying wonder, what injured joy? But she *had* known one thing that night, even before he asked her to marry him and she said yes. She'd known what this, the next and final painting in her Mythic Images series, would be.

She adds a last stroke of burnt sienna to the painting and stands back to examine it. It's her best one so far, and it's ready now, at least this phase of it. Just in time, because it's to be her surprise wedding gift to Biren. She thinks how she'll do it—steal into their new condo the evening before the wedding—she has the key already—and hang it in the foyer so that he will see it first thing when they enter together as husband and wife. Or maybe she'll hang it opposite their bed, so they can look at it after lovemaking, or in

the morning, waking each other up. The tree with its mul-
ticolored jewel leaves, its branches filled with silky birds. It's
the kalpa taru, the wish-fulfilling tree, and the birds are sha-
likhs, those bold, brown creatures she would find everywhere when she visited Calcutta, with their clever pin eyes
and their strident cry. Her grandmother used to call them
birds of memory. Ruchira had meant to ask her why but
never got around to it. Now she doesn't want to ask anyone else. She has given the birds the faces of the people she
loves most dearly. And Biren too—she borrowed one of his
photo albums, secretly, for this purpose. She has put him
and herself, feathers touching, at the very center of the tree.
(Why not? It's her right as artist to be egoistic if she
wants.) Below them she has left empty branches, lots of
them, for the birds she will paint in. New friends, children.
Is it sentimental to be thinking about grandchildren already?
She'll fill every space, and more. Maybe she'll never be
done.

Then Biren's knocking, and she lifts the easel into the
closet and rushes to the door and opens it. But it's not him,
of course not, it's the middle of the afternoon, he's at work.
She really should be more careful and keep the chain on
while she checks who's outside, though this person doesn't
look particularly dangerous. It's a young woman—well,
maybe not so young, once you take in the cracked lines at

the corners of her eyes—very thin and very pregnant, with spiky blond hair and a pierced eyebrow, wearing a shapeless pink smock that looks borrowed and a studded black leather jacket that she can no longer button over her belly. There's a look on her face—determined? resigned? exhilarated? Ruchira gets ready to tell her that she has come to the wrong address. Then she sees it, above the smock's meandering neckline, against the too-pale freckled skin. Red and blue. A bruise, or a half-healed wound. No. It's the hilt of a tattooed knife.

RUCHIRA SITS AWKWARDLY at her kitchen table, knees pressed together, as though she were the visitor here, and stares at the knife-woman. She had realized, right away, that she shouldn't let her in. But she couldn't just shut the door in the face of a pregnant woman who looked like she was starving, could she? It was not, however, a totally altruistic act. Ruchira knows this, though she is unable to articulate what it is that she hopes to gain from Biren's ex-lover. Now she stares at the woman, who is sitting in a chair opposite her and crumbling, with self-possession, the muffin that Ruchira has given her into a small anthill. Ruchira tries to be angry with her for being here. But she feels like someone who drowned a long time ago. In the underwater world she inhabits, there are no emotions, only a slow, seaweedy drifting. She asks, "Why did you come?"

The woman looks up, and the light slip-slides over her hungry cheekbones. What is she hungry for? She's finished demolishing the muffin, but her fingers continue to twitch. Ruchira suspects scars under the leather, puckered fang marks in the dip inside the woman's elbow, the same place she loves to kiss on Biren's arm. Where she has chewed away the lipstick, the woman's lips are papery, like palest cherry blossom. Then she speaks, an unexpected dimple appears in her cheek, and Ruchira is shocked to discover she's beautiful. "My name's Arlene," she says.

Ruchira wants to ask how she knew about her and Biren, about this apartment. Did she see them on Telegraph Avenue, perhaps, late one night, returning from a movie at the Pacific Film Archives? Did she follow them back? Did she watch from the shadows as they kissed under a street-lamp, their hands inside each other's coats? Ruchira wants to ask if she loved him, too.

But she knows enough to wait—it's a game of silences they are playing—and after a while Arlene says, "It'll be born in a month, in February." She narrows her eyes and stares as though Ruchira were a minor fact she's memorizing for a future test, one she'd rather not take.

This time Ruchira loses the game because she can't bear not to know.

"Does he know about the baby?"

"Yes."

Ruchira holds this new, trembling knowledge like a too-heavy blob of paint at the end of a brush, threatening to ruin the entire painting unless she finds the right spot to apply it.

"He gave me the money for an abortion. But I didn't."

Ruchira closes her eyes. The insides of her eyelids are like torn brown silk, like hundreds of birds taking flight at a killing sound. When she opens them, Arlene lifts her shoulders in a shrug. The knife hilt moves up and down over the bumpy bones of her thin chest. The blade is curved in the shape of a Nepali kukri. Ruchira wonders how much it hurt to get the tattoo done, and how the tattooer knew about Nepali knives, and if Arlene ever looked in the mirror and thought of it as a mistake.

"He doesn't know I kept it," Arlene says. She grins suddenly, for the first time, with gamine charm, a kid who's just won at kickball. There's a small, neat gap between her front teeth. A famous poet—who was it?—had proclaimed gap-toothed women to be sexy. Why is it that Ruchira can never remember crucial information when she needs to?

Arlene stands up with a decisive scrape of her chair.

"Wait," Ruchira cries. "Where do you live? Do you have health insurance? Do you need money?" She reaches for her purse and digs frantically in it, coming up with all the bills she can find, ones and fives and a twenty, and extends them to Arlene.

"I'm going to Arizona," says Arlene. She doesn't offer further details. She doesn't stretch out her hand for the money. She does a little pirouette (was she a dancer, before?) and from the door she calls out, "Think of me in February, in Arizona."

THE FIRST THING Ruchira does after she is sure Arlene is gone is to run down the stairs to the garbage area. There it is, next to the Dumpster: the blue recycling bin with its triangle of arrows. In her mind she's seeing the garbage bag, white, with a red tie, that she upended over it—was it just two days back?—freeing a tumble of papers and books. In her mind she's already dug past the discards of other people's lives—term papers and love letters and overdue bills—to grab it. She's opened its purple cover and has started writing, she isn't done writing even when her hand begins to cramp up, she fills her book of errors all the way to the back cover and has more to put down, that's how much she's learned in this one hour.

But the bin is empty.

Ruchira leans into the wall, pressing her forehead

against the fake stucco. It smells of sour milk and diapers, and its bumps leave indentations on her skin. Behind her she hears footsteps approach.

"Arlene," she calls, turning wildly, as though hoping for instructions. But it is a different woman, one of Ruchira's neighbors, who looks vaguely alarmed. She carries a Hefty bag in one hand and holds on to a little boy with the other.

"Mommy," the boy asks, "what's wrong with the lady?"

IT'S VERY LATE now, and Ruchira has packed everything, even the bedsheets, even the pillow. She lies down on the bare mattress and watches the shadows on the wall. She's chilled, but inside her brain it feels hot and spongy. *What would you do, Thakuma?* Inside her brain, her grandmother says, Why do you ask me? Can you live your life the way I lived mine? She speaks with some asperity. Or maybe it's sorrow she feels for the confused world her grand-daughter has inherited. Ruchira recalls a prayer her grand-mother used to chant in the mornings after her bath, in her raspy, sugarcane voice, as she waved a stick of incense in front of the brightly colored pictures on her altar. *Forgive us, O Lord Shiva, all our errors, both the known and the unknown.* It had seemed impossible to Ruchira that her grandmother could commit any errors. Now she knows better, but she is still unsure what those errors might have been. *Errors that took your life between their thumb and forefinger, Thakuma, and crumbled it like a muffin until you were alone, separated by oceans and deserts and a million skyscrapers from the people you loved, and then you were dead.* Ruchira wants to say the old prayer, but she has forgotten most of it. Does a fragmented prayer merit a fragmented forgiveness? On the wall the shadows move like sleepy birds. If there really were a kalpa taru, what would she wish for?

She had called Biren at home and got his answering machine. But how could you tell a machine, You lousy jerk, you son of a bitch, forget about the wedding? How could you explain to metal and plastic why you needed to grasp the promises a man had made to you and break them across the middle, snap-snap, like incense sticks?

At his work, his secretary informed her he was at a lunch meeting. Could she call back in an hour?

No, she could not. She rummaged through her phone book. Here it was, his cell phone number, written in his expansive, looped hand.

On this machine, his voice sounded huskier, sexy in a businesslike way. Against her will, she found herself listening as he asked people to leave a message at the tone. But the tone didn't come on just yet. Instead, the voice said, "And in case this is Ruchira, I want you to know I'm crazy about you."

There were three short, impatient beeps. She held the phone pressed to her ear until the machine disconnected her. He hadn't informed her about that voice mail greeting, which was a kind of public avowal of his love. He trusted that one day, at the right time, she would find out.

Was that trust enough to outweigh a lifetime of imagining, each time she kissed Biren, that Arlene's papery lips had bloomed there already? He had never pretended Ruchira was his first. How could she blame him for a past he had admitted to right at the start, just because it had come to her door wearing a pierced eyebrow, an implosive, elfish smile? And the baby, smooth and oval in its ivory sheath, its head pushing up against the echo of a knife. The error its father had paid to erase. She couldn't blame Biren for that either. Could she?

She won't tell Biren about Arlene and the baby. Ruchira knows this as she watches the shadows detach themselves from her walls to flap their way across the ceiling. And she won't be sad for him. The baby, she means. A boy. She knows this inside herself as surely as though she were his mother. A boy—she whispers this to herself—named Arizona. There are many ways in the world to love. With luck he'll find one. And with luck Ruchira will, too. But what is she thinking? She already loves Biren. Isn't that why all evening she has been folding and stuffing and tearing strips of tape and printing words on brown cartons in aggressive black ink? *Books: living room. China: dining alcove.* Their lives are already mixed, like past and future, promise and disappointment, linseed oil and turpentine. Like the small exhalations of birds on a wish-fulfilling tree. Maybe they can be separated, but she doesn't have the expertise for it, even if she wanted to. Marriage is a long, hobbled race, learning the other's gait as you go, and thanks to Arlene she has a head start.

The wind has dropped. On Ruchira's window sill the shadows lie stunned, as though they've been shot. She wonders if Biren and Arlene did drugs together. It wouldn't have been a needle, he was too fastidious for that. Maybe pills. Ecstasy? Dexedrine? It annoys her suddenly that she doesn't know enough about these things. *Clothes: master bedroom. Medicines: bathroom cabinet. Paints: studio.* Because Biren wants her to have a studio in their new condo, on the airy top floor with its view of Coit Tower, next to the balcony where they're planning to sit in the evenings and drink jasmine tea and talk. (But what will they talk about?) Until one day in February the wind will be like cherry blosssoms, and she'll take down the painting she hung in the foyer and go into the studio and add in a bird with a boy-face and spiky gold hair, with Biren's square chin and an unsuspected dimple. And if Biren asks about him . . . ? This is what Ruchira wants from the kalpa taru: that when Biren asks, she'll know how to ask him back.

THE NAMES OF STARS
IN BENGALI

THE CHILDREN LOVED the bamboo forest behind the house. That's what they all called it, even the adults, bansh-ban, bamboo forest, though *thicket* would have been a more suitable word for the modest clumps that separated the house from the neighbor's pond. And yet there *was* something forestlike in the way the bamboo shoots poked the dark, intent sharpness of their leaves closer and closer to the house, even into it, through the bars of the dining room window. Something instinctive, predatory, and the children, who were four and five, felt it. It made them open their blue eyes very wide and jump up and down with a wild, adrenaline thrill, chanting the old folk rhyme their grandmother had taught them, bansh boner kaché, burho shial naché, which she had explained was about foxes dancing in a bamboo forest. They didn't know much Bengali, and the words came out of their mouths wrongly accented, making all the adults laugh. The adults were their grandmother, their great-uncle, his wife, and the servant-woman, who all lived in the house, and any neighbor ladies who happened to drop by to see the little Americans, as they called the boys. They were all wonderfully ancient and wore long, drapey clothes and moved floatingly, as though through an invisible lake. Like very wise elephants, the older boy said to the younger one. Even their smiles took a long time to form, and then stayed on their faces forever, until the children couldn't tell them apart from their wrinkles.

The adults also included their mother. But was it really their mother, this woman who had put away the jeans and T-shirts they were familiar with and now wore a blue-striped sari and a dusty red dot in the middle of her forehead? They liked the change. She seemed younger and foreign and laughed more than at home and ate with her hands, expertly deboning a lethal-looking catfish while they watched with fascinated repulsion. She wasn't in a hurry all the time, jangling her car keys and saying, Let's *go*, boys, come *on*, boys, we're late al*ready*. The second day they'd

been in the village, she'd stopped at the all-purpose store
and bought a dozen bangles of silvery glass, and these made
a faint windy music around her wherever she went. She reminded them of the characters in the stories their grandmother told them nightly in the dark.

Which one? the mother asked, smiling, when the
younger boy told her this. The princess, I hope? The boy
shook his head and said it was the farmer's youngest daughter-in-law, the clever one who saves the family because she
knows the language of animals.

That was their favorite time, just before sleep, in their
grandmother's narrow widow's bed. They pressed against
the buttery, pleated skin of her arms, interrupting whenever
she lapsed into Bengali, what does it mean, Didima, what
does it mean, until she would call across the dark room to
their mother, Really, Khuku, you've got to do a better job
teaching these children their mother tongue. That always
made them hysterical with laughter, because Khuku meant
baby girl, they knew that much. Next morning they'd make
fun of her, calling, Khuku, Khuku, take us for a bath in
the pond, and she'd pretend to get mad and say, I'll khuku
your behinds if you don't show some respect right now.
Then they'd laugh again, they hadn't laughed so much in
their entire lives, they'd never thought India would be
this much fun, they wished they could stay forever.

When they said that, both their mother and grand-mother grew quiet and didn't answer.

In the middle of the bedtime story, the grandmother would stop and say, Hush, children, listen to the foxes, and they would all listen—first the raucous sawing of the crickets, then the asthmatic whistle of a passing train, then the bamboo leaves, secretive, like dry palms rubbed together, and, finally, faint and mournful with distance, the hua-hua of the foxes rising thin and smoky in the dark. The sound made a hot, scratchy feeling happen in their chests, like hooks pulling. It became impossible to lie still. They bounced around in the bed, they knew they would explode otherwise. The old wood let out complaining moans, but the grandmother didn't scold them. It was as if she, too, knew that feeling.

As soon as the story was done, the grandmother would grab them, one ankle in each hand, and say, Now, boys, no running off to your ma. You have to sleep with me tonight. This, too, was part of the ritual. They giggled and slip-slided their feet from her grasp, blew her loud kisses, and felt their way across the shadowy room to their mother. A mattress had been laid down for them on the cool floor, which during the day was a pale-green mosaic flecked with silver. Like fish fins, the younger boy had told the older one. They burrowed into their mother's body, its damp, grassy smells. When they went back to America, they weren't ever going to sleep in their own beds alone, without her. They'd already decided that between themselves. They put their heads on her pillow, one on each side, and listened as she talked to the grandmother. They mostly didn't understand the words, and that was fine. Sometimes happy, sometimes sad, the women's voices flowed over them like melted ice cream, Häagen-Dazs vanilla, their favorite flavor, and their father's as well. Thinking of their father caused a small noose of sorrow to tighten around them. But they wriggled from it easily. They'd all be together again before they knew it, he'd said, kissing them good-bye in San Francisco. Meanwhile, the village was the greatest adventure of their lives.

AT THE POND, her sari lifted discreetly to her knees, the mother dangles her feet in the moss-green water and watches the children splashing around. Soon the sun will grow uncomfortably hot. But for the moment the brick steps that lead down to the pond are lazily, familiarly warm under her thighs. In her muscles she feels a memory struggling to wake. This same pleasant end-of-winter glow seeping through frock and knickers into her skin, her father's hands firm around hers, smelling of cinnamon. (Why cinnamon, she has no idea. He had been no cook, her father. Never set foot in the kitchen if he could avoid it.) He was helping her hold a homemade fishing rod. Did they do this more than once? Did they catch anything? She cannot recall, and this fills her with an absurd sense of loss.

She had been worried about making this trip to India—her first since the boys were born—without her husband. But they both agreed it was important to do it this way. To have him along—even if he could have spared the six weeks from his job—would have changed the ambience of her homecoming. Because though her mother had written a separate letter asking him to come, he was an outsider. No matter how much she loved him, she knew that.

The only time he'd visited India was for the wedding, which had turned out to be a stony-lipped, rushed affair, with just a few relatives attending. It took place in a squalid courthouse in Calcutta with sooty windows and a fan that didn't work and a long corridor which smelled like rancid fruit, where they'd had to wait a long time. They'd been forced to come to this dismal place, like runaways, because none of the priests in the village would conduct the marriage. They had asked her husband if he was Hindu, and he had replied he wasn't, although he held the religion in high esteem. But your father is Hindu, right? they asked, offering him one last chance. To which he replied with American frankness that his father, though born a Hindu, had stopped practicing the religion long before he married his white, Episcopalian wife.

Waiting in the corridor of the courtroom, her aunt—her father's sister—had said, It's a good thing your father isn't alive to see this day. Shocked and stung, the daughter turned to her mother, expecting her to come to her rescue. But her mother merely looked down at the grimy floor, and the daughter realized that she, too, believed this.

The trip from California to Calcutta had been long and exhausting, every bit as bad as she had feared. Each time she needed to use the bathroom, the boys had insisted on accompanying her, even into the minuscule airplane stall. In Heathrow airport, they'd run off around the corner while she was busy at the passport counter, and for a few terrifying minutes she thought she'd lost them. When in desperation she belted them into the double stroller they considered themselves too grown up for, the older one pulled the younger one's hair, and the younger one bit him hard enough to leave a ragged half-moon of tooth marks on his arm. Then they both cried so energetically that passersby stopped to shoot her disapproving glances, until finally the mother had to resort to taking a Valium.

But it was worth every bit of trouble, she thinks now, as she watches them splash about in waist-deep water, pretending to swim. Mostly they whoop and churn up mud. How well they got along with her mother, right from the first. And her mother—more than anything else, she was amazed at her own mother. The hours she spent listening to knock-knock jokes which must have made no sense to her, the hours she spent making them elaborate snacks which they quite often refused to eat. They showed her their comic books and told her in dramatic detail about their favorite superheroes. They tied a handkerchief over her eyes and made her play blind man's buff with them. She had never been this patient with her own daughter, the mother thinks, stung by a small resentment. Then she is ashamed.

The boys have scared off the ducks, who are clumped under the dark-splotched taro leaves at the other end of the pond, quacking indignantly. The servant boy who is in the water with them—in case they slip or wander too deep—flaps his elbows like wings and quacks back in a nasal falsetto that sets the boys off again into fits of squirmy laughter. The servant boy annoys the mother. Perhaps it is because she had to bring him to watch the boys even though she is a good swimmer herself. But she isn't confident about how well she would do in a sari, six waterlogged yards of cotton pulling her down, and of course in the village a swimsuit is out of the question. She hasn't even brought one, she doesn't want to cause trouble, not during this visit. There has been enough trouble in her past already.

This time the memory comes as a sensation on her skin. She is as old as the servant boy—twelve, perhaps—swimming across the pond in her frock and knickers. She has tucked up the skirt so she can swim better. It sloshes pouchlike against her stomach, makes her feel ancient and marsupial. Ahead, the water stretches out forever, a veritable sea—the way her children must be seeing it now. But she is not afraid. She will never tire. Tiny bubbles of rainbow air wink from her arm when she lifts it for a stroke.

There was an incident. She has forgotten the details by now. She only remembers the boys waiting by the road, smoking beedis as she returned home from the pond. That sour, wild stench, those thin corkscrews of smoke. They'd shouted comments, made vulgar kissing sounds, though she had been careful to wrap a large towel around her frocked-and-knickered body. She had run home, her heart rattling like a stone inside a box that someone shook and shook. It was her first encounter with terror.

When her mother heard—in the village, you always heard—she had put an end to the swimming. Even though the girl had wept and pleaded and refused to eat for two days and said she would only go in a group with the other girls. But there *were* no other girls, her mother pointed out, reasonably enough. Good families didn't let grown girls swim in ponds so everyone could ogle them. This was true. So the girl took her rage and sank it in her chest, where it waited like a cylinder of radioactive waste deep beneath the ocean. Everyone thought she'd accepted her mother's decree. But she was gathering her strength for the next confrontation.

Sitting on the pond steps, the mother thinks her way back to her teenage self, the secret hardness growing inside her. The day she would finally reveal it, it would shock everyone—as though they'd sliced open a ripe papaya to find a rock inside. Because all this time they'd thought her pleasantly quiet and studious, changed for the better. Such a sober girl, they said in admiration. She had stopped going to the village fair with her schoolmates. She was no longer interested in the plays performed by visiting troupes in the marketplace. In class she knew all the right answers. She asked the librarian if she could borrow the fat, dusty tomes, math and science, that none of the other girls ever looked at. A termite-gnawed copy of Shakespeare. She read them from beginning to end. Sometimes after school she went to the headmistress's home to discuss the more complex sections with her. This was not because of a love for learning. Already she knew this about herself. She read with ruthless concentration, the way one studies code in wartime.

Somewhere hidden in the books, she knew, lay the theorem of her escape, the formula for the life she craved. Somewhere there was a soliloquy she could appropriate as her own.

When she had passed her higher secondary exams with the highest marks in the district, she went to the headmistress and told her she wanted to go to college in Calcutta, and asked her to speak to her parents. She knew that her parents, however reluctant, would not be able to refuse the headmistress. They would be intimidated by her position, her horn-rimmed glasses and earnest, temple-gong voice as she spoke of the girl's talent and what a crime it would be to waste it, especially now that she'd been awarded a government scholarship, such a coup for their little village school. No, no, the parents with their old-fashioned notions mustn't stand in her way.

It was a betrayal, doing it like this. The girl knew it, and her parents, too. They spoke of it bitterly after the headmistress left. There was shouting, accusations, her mother implored her to reconsider. Finally she was sent to her room. She lay in bed, her mouth dry, her head pounding, staring up at the ceiling. Her life was shifting—tectonic plates colliding, fissures opening up. The evening light was grainy and saffron, a color she'd never noticed because she'd never lain idly in bed at this time of day. Downstairs, she could hear her mother weeping. There was a noise like a door being slammed. The sounds distressed and elated her at the same time. She knew her parents couldn't go back on their word to the headmistress. She would go to college, she would live with guilt. That was okay. Guilt was easier to live with than regret.

Now she blinks, disoriented by heat and recollection. Where are the boys? For a moment so frightening that her voice is frozen in her throat, there are only striations of wind on water. She plunges in to her waist, her hands shaking as they search the water, which is blacker and colder than she'd imagined. But they've surfaced already to the side of her, all three of them, from some kind of submarine game, blowing out great mouthfuls of water like whales, laughing.

Boys! she gasps. Out! Right now! She grasps each of her sons by his bony forearm and gives him a shake. She glares at the servant boy. You were supposed to keep them safe, she tells him, not make more trouble. And, boys, didn't I say over and over, no pond water in your mouth? Why do you think your grandma's been boiling water for you every day, even to brush your teeth? It's germy, that's why. Full of little, slimy germs too small to see.

All the excited joy drains from her sons' bodies. Their blue eyes—so disconcerting in their sun-browned faces—fill with tears. She hates herself for this, but she can't stop. And worms, she says, teeny, tiny worms with hooks that dig into your flesh. Her wet sari clings to her legs as she starts for home, it rasps her skin with its edge of gathered gravel. Ahead of her, the boys' backs shake with suppressed sobs. What a witch she is, worse than the baby-eating rakkushi in the stories her mother tells them. She touches their bony boy-shoulders with compunctious fingers, she wants to gather them back inside her, into her own childhood, she wants time to reverse and simplify itself. She wants to tell them they are loved. Instead she hears herself saying, And mosquito eggs, too, which are probably hatching right this minute in your stomachs.

IN THE EVENINGS, they held court.

When a garnet sun had slipped behind the black spikes of bamboo, and the veranda had been sprinkled with water to cool it for the guests, the maidservant would set off for Kesto's Sweet Shop to fetch fresh-fried jilipis and singaras. The children were allowed to go with her, but only after they promised they wouldn't eat anything offered to them by the street vendors. It was hard. All along the bazaar, men would smile and beckon, speaking a mix of Bengali and broken English, words they'd picked up from the movies,

Come, come, little American babus, try one-two sandesh, free for you, try pani-puri, I make for you no chilies, try very sweet lozenges. The candy gleamed up at them like happy jewels from their tray of dusted sugar. The pani-puris were precariously balanced brown balls, crisp, light as air. Oh, it was too cruel to have to leave it all behind. When they had children, the boys promised each other, they would never do this to them.

The first visitors to arrive were always the widows. They perched on folding chairs on the cooled veranda. In their hushed white saris, they were like great moths. They balanced their teacups expectantly on their knees and took slow sips. They had all the time in the world. Then came the older wives who had daughters-in-law at home to make dinner, fresh from their evening shower, smelling of Cuticura talcum powder. Stacks of gold bangles, generations of dowry, clanked on their arms. The red marriage mark in the cleft of their hair gleamed like a triumphant wound. Finally, a few men with canes and flashlights, mostly the great-uncle's friends, who had to break their singaras into little pieces and gum them for a long time. Once the younger boy paused his game with his Batman and Robin action figures to ask why all the men were so old. The mother put her hand over his mouth. Later she explained it was because it was not proper for young men to visit a woman whose husband wasn't there. The older boy scrunched his forehead and drew in a fierce, interrogative breath, but she forestalled him. That's just how it is in the village, she said.

The visitors asked many questions about America. Usually they were the same ones. Is it true you have machines that do all your housework? Is it true that a pound of mangoes can cost as much as a watch from Taiwan? Is it true everyone drives a car, even the old people? Is it true that when the old people can't drive their cars anymore, their children put them into nursing homes?

The mother didn't know what to say. A simple yes or no, wrenched out of context, would give them such a wrong impression of America. It would be dishonest. How could she tell them about her blender and vacuum cleaner and clothes dryer without explaining how at the end of the day she rushed home from work (her computer with its psychedelic screen-saver at which she sometimes stared, zombie-eyed, for chunks of time), picking up the children on the way, stopping at the grocery if they were out of milk. How the boys insisted on hanging from the edge of the grocery cart in exactly the way the little red warning sign on it said not to. How they whined for Gummi Worms. Or how, late at night, the boys asleep and her husband also, she would get up to wash after sex—she was finicky that way, even when the sex was good—and hear the dishwasher running. Its squat, urgent hum pulled at something inside her. It made her walk all the way to the kitchen and lean into it. It throbbed under her palm. In all the world, she and it seemed the only things left alive.

This had always been her problem, the inability to explain to those back home the texture of an alien life. When her parents had asked how it was to live in the Manimala Debi Girls' Hostel in Calcutta, she had wanted to speak of the dull oppression of the ancient gray building, its sweating cement walls, its unending rules. The way her dinner would be left for her on the kitchen table, drying rice, congealed dal, covered with a net mesh to keep the cockroaches out, if she stayed too long at the library. But what of the triangular terrace, its hot, hard canopy of sky? From this terrace she could see the junction of Shyam Bajar, the nonstop bustle of hawkers and pedestrians that filled the space between them and her with a sparking, combustible energy. Maimed beggars pulled themselves along on small wooden boards with wheels. At lunchtime they gathered in the shade of a movie billboard and made raucous jokes, pointing at the bosomy film stars that loomed over them. A pickpocket was caught and beaten up by the crowd. Schoolgirls in white and brown uniforms, carrying the tricolor flag, marched in a parade every August 15, followed amicably by

a Communist group waving militant red banners and shouting, in call-and-response fashion, *Jyoti Basu zindabad, Congress
Party murdabad.* Ambulances made their tortuous, clanging
way through rickshaws and cows, bearing the dying who
sometimes expired before reaching the hospital. Men pro-
testing the hike in the price of tickets burned a bus; the
smoke rose in chemical gusts as the red paint on its sides
melted to black. In seeing, she became part of it all. It was
as much her education as the classes and the books.

I like college, she had replied to her parents. I miss
home. I have a quiet roommate. I have no trouble studying.
I am careful not to miss curfew. You've seen my exam re-
sults, they're good. She waited guiltily for them to chastise
her for prevarication. But they nodded, went on to other
matters. Amazed, she realized they hadn't wanted to hear
anything else.

So now she told the visitors, Yes, there were two cars
in her family, one for her husband, one for herself. They
nodded. We knew it, we knew it, they said to her mother.
Land of gold. Your Khuku is living like a queen. They
looked so happily envious, so vindicated in their rightness,
that she didn't have the heart to say anything about the high
insurance rates, or the drivers who cut her off during rush
hour, or honked and yelled, Fucking Dothead go home. The
time she'd had a flat tire on the freeway and stood there,

frozen by the deafening metallic shapes hurtling past her, meteorlike, for an entire half hour until an old Chinese man stopped to help her. How could she explain to them that she would have preferred to take buses—only, there weren't any.

She liked it better when the visitors spoke about old times, times beyond her remembering. When the village was a small clearing among forests of mango and shal. Before the railroads even, before electricity, when the village doctor had to travel to his patients on a bullock cart with kerosene lamps dangling from it, and new brides were sent to their in-laws' homes in covered palanquins. Sometimes a woman would disappear while washing clothes in the dighi, and it was whispered that the water spirit had taken her. During the independence movement the swadeshis hid from the British forces in the surrounding forests and built their bombs in an old brick pit less than a mile from here. Bandits lived in the forests too, and preyed on travelers. They wore gold earrings and painted their faces with lampblack to avoid being recognized. Because they didn't really live in the forest. They lived right here in the village. They might have been your next-door neighbors. Once a brahmin went for a bath in the river and felt something scrape his arm, hard as teeth. Inspired by divine courage, he grasped it—it was a stone statue of Goddess Durga, the one you see in the temple by the bazaar, to whom children who are seriously ill are taken for blessing. But now, just look around, everyone and his brother has a TV antenna sticking out from his thatched roof, and the boys on the street are whistling tunes from American rock stars, even though they don't understand the ingrezi words. Hai, where has our culture gone?

The mother fell into the tales, let their current take her. She wanted desperately to believe them, to believe that through them she was learning back her past, what to pass on to her children. What America had leached away from her. In the years of drought, the zamindar threw open his granary. His wife cooked khichuri for the starving peasants with her own hands. His daughters served them on banana leaf platters. The mother closed her eyes and smelled the feast, the peppery stew of rice and lentils, potato and cauliflower, raisins imported all the way from Afghanistan. If the tales were no truer than those woven about America, how you went there penniless and in two years you owned a chain of motels, she—not unlike her parents all those years ago—didn't want to know.

THE YOUNGER BOY has fallen sick. It begins as a pain in his stomach, a slight nausea, and the mother puts him on toast and bottled Limca, bought from the most expensive

store in the village to guarantee that it hasn't been adulter-
ated. The nausea ends, but the stomachache is worse, and
when he goes to the bathroom there are only spurts of
flecked brown water. He cries constantly. Kaopectate
doesn't help, nor Immodium, and Children's Tylenol only
reduces him to a glazed whimpering. Worried, the mother
starts him on antibiotics. The wrenching bowel motions
continue; soon he's too weak to run about. He lies on his
side and stares at the barred rectangle of yellow light from
the window. He hates the taste of Limca and cries for 7-Up
and his father. From time to time, in a tone of exhausted
anger, he demands pepperoni pizza.

At night, the mother can't sleep. They've moved the
sick boy's mattress to the passage near the bathroom for
easy access, and she lies next to him on a pallet, her hand
on his clammy forehead, checking his temperature. Her
older son has finally fallen asleep in her mother's bed—after throwing a huge tantrum at being separated from his
brother. She can hear her mother's uneven breathing next
door and knows that she, too, is awake, but she is too de-
pressed to talk to her. The village doctor came earlier and
replaced the American antibiotic with an Indian one. Better
for our desi germs, he said. It is a bitter puce mixture, and
her son keeps pushing it away. When it's medicine-time, the
maidservant has to hold his arms while the mother forces

open his mouth and his brother, who has been sitting outside the door of the sickroom all day, sobs in outraged sympathy. Afterward, both boys look at her with loathing. The
women are urging her to get a herb poultice from the medicine man in the next village. Also, she must take the boy
to Durga's shrine tomorrow, without fail. The goddess is
very powerful. Kesto's daughter had typhoid last year, baap
re, what fever, the doctor said he couldn't do anything more.
Then they took her and put her at the deity's feet—and the
next day she was sitting up asking for food. But maybe she
has become American and stopped believing in such things?

The mother wishes she knew the right thing to do.
Uncertainties line her stomach like ulcers, a constant, dull
ache. She doesn't trust poultices, which she remembers
from her own childhood as slimy, foul-smelling, and of little efficacy. She's afraid the boy is too weak to be dragged
to any temple. She isn't convinced that Indian antibiotics
are better than American ones. She wonders (yes, that's how
weak-minded she's grown) if she called a curse down on her
son that day by the pond, going on and on about hook-
worms and mosquito eggs. Oh, she should never have
brought them to India, just to assuage the guilt she felt at
depriving her mother of her grandchildren.

The mother wants to cry in great unrestrained sobs but
knows she must not. Everyone in the house is depending

on her—as though they were her children too, she thinks in sudden anger. For three days she's been trying to call her husband, but the phone lines are not working. Finally she asked her second uncle's son to go to the post office and send a telegram. Maybe it has gone to the wrong address. Maybe it hasn't gone at all. Maybe the postal employee only pretended to send it and pocketed the money. Why isn't her husband here, the one time she needs him, she thinks with a rage she recognizes as irrational. But she feels entitled to her irrationality, anyone would be, after four nights of no sleep, and almost no food. Her mother keeps nagging at her to eat, but how *can* she when her son is dehydrating right before her eyes, his arms turning into knobby sticks, the skin around his mouth dusty and brittle like the earth in a year of no rain? She casts around in her mind for someone to blame. None of this would have happened if her mother hadn't been so stubborn about never visiting America again.

THREE YEARS AFTER her marriage. Five years after her father's death. That was when the daughter finally managed to persuade her mother to come and visit her. But from the first it was a mistake. Her mother, an inviolable presence in the village, moving galleon-like inside the voluminous white

yardage of her widow's sari, had turned fearful and queru-
lous in America. Things the daughter saw as inconsequen-
tial—the burglar alarm, the answering machine, the knobs
on the dishwasher—loomed like huge, barbed obstacles on
her daily horizon.

They fought about silly things—how to make a cauliflower curry, what is better for hair, shampoo-and-condi-
tioner or coconut-oil-and-ritha pulp. They argued bitterly
about events from years back. Her mother claimed she had
taken the daughter to the Alipore zoo on a particular birthday, waking early to fry luchis for lunch, taking the train all
the way to Calcutta. The daughter remembered none of it.
She insinuated that her parents had never engaged in fun
activities as a family. Fun! her mother scoffed. What a foolish American notion! Families were not for fun. They were
for feeding and clothing and teaching children, so that they
would, in turn, be adequately equipped to feed and clothe
and teach *their* children. At the ends of these arguments, one
or the other of them would flounce from the room on the
verge of tears.

I can't believe we're behaving like this, fighting over
such trivial things, the daughter told her husband at night
in vexed disbelief. It's like she's turned me into a child again.
But of course what they were fighting about was not trivial—it was an entire geography (real and imagined), endan-

gered by the knowledge of new things, by the transformation of desire.

Her husband listened attentively, fixing her with his dark, calm gaze (he had not inherited his mother's blue eyes, which would surface only in his children). He was sympathetic, and often drove his mother-in-law to the homes of other Bengalis with older relatives. Otherwise, he wisely refrained from offering advice. Born in America, what could he have said, anyway? His filial duties were few, and geometric in their clarity. His parents lived forty miles away in their own home. They were both in good health and drove themselves wherever they needed to go: the grocery, the Rotary Club, concerts at the Julia Morgan Theater. They had already picked out a senior citizens' facility they both liked, within walking distance of the beach, in Santa Cruz. He and his wife met them each Sunday for brunch at Mumtaz, which offered an excellent but not too spicy Indian buffet, but if something else came up, his parents didn't mind rescheduling. Even his father, who in recent years had reverted to a number of Indian habits, such as not wearing shoes in the house and eating rice with his fingers, was relaxed that way.

Coming home from work, the daughter would, each day, call out to her mother. One day there was no answer. Concerned, she ran up to the guest room and found her mother lying on her side, eyes closed, breathing shallowly. The skin on her face, leached of its usual almond sheen, was puffy and whitish, like the skin of an ocean creature that has been removed from its habitat. The daughter put her hand on her mother's feet. They were very cold. Mother, she called again, this time in fear. Her father had died like this, turning on to his side one afternoon after lunch, a year after she left for America. Mother! Finally, without opening her eyes, her mother said, Khuku, send me home.

The daughter sat by her mother for a long time, massaging her feet. They did not talk, though they wept a little. They were coming to terms with erosion, how it changes the balance of a landscape. Perhaps it was something all parents and children undergo as they grow older. But in their case, they had stepped into a time machine named immigration, and when they fell from its ferocious spinning, it was into the alien habits of a world they had imagined imperfectly. In this world, they could not inhabit a house together, in the old way. They could not be mother and daughter in that way again.

THE CHILDREN'S FATHER has, miraculously, arrived. But how did he find his way from the Calcutta airport to this village, which, though loved by its inhabitants, is after all small and undistinguished? I gave a man some money to be my guide, he says. The visitors—the room is full of them, male and female, young and old, relatives and neighbors— suck in their collectively horrified breath. Durga! Durga! He could have been led astray and mugged, maybe even killed. Because in spite of his brown skin anyone could see he was a foreigner, with his pockets full of dollars. He nods, clearly not understanding, and smiles a trusting, foreigner smile.

The father is wearing loose white pants and a white kurta belonging to the great-uncle, a fact which fills the children with hilarity. There is a whole posse of them in the corner, his older son, the servant's boy, a neighbor's child, two girls belonging to his wife's cousin-brother. They whisper breathlessly about how, when he received the telegram, he hadn't taken the time to pack anything except two cases of 7-Up and three boxes of Nabisco saltine crackers (a baggage that has already begun to take on the status of legend) for his sick child. That's why he's wearing the great-uncle's clothes, they explain to each other. They observe him with wide, wondering eyes as though he were a minor god.

The younger boy is much better now. He sits on his father's lap and accepts the attention that is lavished on him like a prince who has been discovered while traveling incognito. When he looks up at the geckos on the wall, his eyes gleam a startling blue. In a few minutes he will squirm away to play Chu-kit-kit with the others, and a casual on-looker, gazing out on the courtyard, will not be able to tell his black head from theirs. Is his improvement due to his father's presence, or to the 7-Up, several cans of which he has drunk already, or to the puja that has been performed in his name at the Durga temple? Each visitor has his or her own view on this, and expresses it loudly and simulta-neously. There is, in the room, a general air of holiday, aided by the many cups of tea that have been consumed, along with a very hot chanachur mix made of fried lentils, flat-tened rice, and a combination of spices that is known only to the grandmother. The visitors exclaim with amazed pleas-ure at how the jamai (that's what they all call him, jamai, son-in-law) munches this lethal snack like a born Bengali, how he pours his steaming tea into his saucer to cool it—just like they would have done, had they not been restrained by his presence.

The mother sits in a corner and observes all this with mingled happiness and chagrin. After all her worrying, how easy her husband is in her childhood home. He has charmed the grandmother, she could see that when he rose to take from her hands the cup of tea she had brought for him. He dipped his head in a little bow—a gesture of old courtesy rarely seen nowadays, and the grandmother flushed with pleasure and said, Long life to you, baba. How intently he listens to the men, who discuss convoluted Calcutta politics, lapsing often into fist-pounding Bengali. How carefully he holds his son and strokes his cheek from time to time. A great and pleasant tiredness has come upon her, and she welcomes it. She could sleep for weeks—she *will* sleep for weeks, now that her husband is here. She feels—as she sometimes does after she has drunk a glass or two of good wine—that she is being borne up inside a rainbow-colored bubble from which she can sense, only remotely, the vibrations of activity around her.

Then her husband turns to her and says, It's such a nice evening, you've been shut up in the house so long, why don't you go with your cousin for a spin on his scooter?

BY THE TIME they finally get away, after the children have been appeased by being taken for rides around the pond, the sun has dwindled to a few slivers of light among the bamboo. But never fear, the cousin-brother informs her. He has a head lamp. And off they go with a roar, raising more dust than an entire herd of cows.

Though the mother has, in her wild, premotherly past, been bungee-jumping and even skydiving, she has never had the occasion to ride on a scooter. She feels nervous and bashful as she sits sideways, the way the cousin has instructed, her feet precariously balanced on a tiny footrest, her sari tucked tight between her knees. She grips the back of his seat with both hands. The wind hits her face in great, cold sheets, making her eyes water. She is afraid that the shawl she has borrowed from her mother to drape around her shoulders will fly off and be lost. There are ruts in the road. Whenever they hit one, which is often, the scooter bounces up, then lands with a thump that jars her backbone. But she is enjoying this, an adventure she didn't plan for. She wants to say something about its serendipitous charm, but how can anyone think in all this exuberance of noise and dust and mongrels chasing after them and children yelling and passers by staring in envious disapproval!

They have taken a route she does not know, a wide, tarmac road curving along the far circumference of the village. The cousin slows down and points at a structure. Tractor shop, she hears him announce above the sputtering of the scooter. Mine. She stares at a large, locked shed with an assortment of machines that hulk inside the wire fencing. Above, in bright red Bengali letters is written JAI KALI TRACTOR FACTORY. Are most of the fields cultivated by tractors now? she asks. He nods vigorously. But what happened to the buffaloes? He shrugs. His shrug implies that only those who come from Coca-Cola Land can afford to ask such esoteric questions. All the tractor owners in the area must come to him for maintenance, he goes on to explain with some pride. He's the only game in town.

The mother remembers snippets of overheard conversation. This cousin had graduated from college only to find—like so many of his generation in Bengal—that there were no jobs for him. He had spent some months lounging on the verandal of the library building, where frustrated young men gathered to curse the corruption of political leaders. It is a tradition that still continues. Even during this visit, the mother has seen a group of men leaning against the lime-washed library wall, arguing and spitting expertly into the drain. The smoke from their beedis had hung around them, gray as an old mosquito net. How had her cousin broken out of that ring of hopelessness? She tries to recall heroic moments out of their childhood games which might help her understand his transformed life, but all she remembers is the time when a lizard had slithered up his foot and caused him to burst into tears. How does one remake oneself, she wants to know. It is a skill she has need of. But she cannot think of an appropriate way of asking this in Bengali.

It is dark now, and the scooter's headlight throws a single beam along the road's brown spine. They are passing mustard fields, she can tell by the pungent odor. The smells of childhood stay with you all your life. Now the deep pink fragrance of madhabi flowers. They must be near the ruins of the Radha-Krishna temple. Now the dense, distinctive smell of manure, which signals a cow barn. She has brought her children halfway across the world to teach them these smells. But for them childhood will probably mean the scent of pepperoni pizza.

The village is changing, the cousin says. You must not think we live like simpletons. Every night my wife and I watch national news on the Door Darshan channel. We know about America, too. O. J. Simpson, Madonna, Monica Lewinsky. How your president sent bombers to the Gulf. The mother tries to figure out if he is chiding her, but his voice is friendly, informational. His hair smells familiar. It takes her a moment to recall the brand, Dabur Amla, the same medicinal oil her father used. Look, he says, here is a new go-down, refrigerated so stored crops will not rot in the monsoon. It has its own generator, in case of power failure. The mother looks obediently at the long, ugly concrete structure, lit at both ends by naked bulbs. A watchman, his nose and mouth wrapped in a faded plaid muffler, sits on a stool, dozing. Her eyes swim away toward the stars. They are a pale yellow, like sprinkled sandalwood powder. Her father used to know their names. *Ashwini, Bharani, Kritika, Rohini.* He had tried to teach her, but she was too busy trying to leave. A night fog is rising from the ground, so that they seem to be traveling between earth and sky. Above the phut-phut of the scooter, she thinks she hears the musky call of foxes. Why should the sound fill her with such elation? When her father died, her mother packed his books into a green trunk filled with mothballs and had it carried into the storage space under the staircase. Maybe there's a book in there, listing the names of stars in Bengali and explaining how to identify them, which she can read to her husband and children. As soon as she gets home, she will ask her mother. She leans forward until her mouth is close to the cousin's ear. Faster, she says. Faster.